The First Abduction

&

The Last Settlers

Prequels to
The Regonia Chronicles

By Elexis Bell

Eager to stay up to date on the latest dark fiction from Elexis Bell?

Sign up for her newsletter on her website. www.elexisbell.com

The First Abduction

By Elexis Bell
Prequel to The Regonia Chronicles

Author's Note:

While writing this short story, I listened to a song called "Can you hold me" by NF. You don't have to listen to that song to get the full effect of the story, but in case you want that extra sensory experience, that's the song I'd recommend.

The stars flicker beyond the circular window, blinking out, one by one. The rogue asteroid moves toward us, slow and certain, stealing the heavens from our view, stealing the breath from my lungs.

How long until it hits?

Beside me, Francois gapes. He reaches out, wrapping his hand around mine. Our suits make the gesture awkward, but it doesn't matter.

I need this last bit of comfort, this last glimpse of humanity.

I need this.

I squeeze his hand, holding on for dear life.

My mouth goes dry as Minister Chekov, our Coalition Representative, speaks over the speakers throughout the station. "We don't have enough fuel left. Our boosters can't push us out of its path unless we use Terata's gravity to do some of the work. We can try, but it'll take time to fire everything up. It might hit before we can move."

Silence falls, and my heart plummets.

Can we survive the hit?

I stare out at the massive rock hurtling toward us at a snail's pace. I run through a million scenarios in my mind, calculating the losses we can withstand. I analyze our life support systems, already faltering thanks to their age.

We could board our smaller ships and go down to Terata. We don't have enough materials mined from the surrounding asteroids to really settle there yet though.

"We gave it a good run," Chekov says, voice breaking over the speakers. "We…"

I step forward, tugging Francois along with me. Putting my free hand to the window, I gape at the rogue asteroid. My eyes dart to the stable ones floating around behind it, to the mining equipment we've deposited on some of the larger ones, glimmering in the faint sunlight.

But the rogue moves closer, blocking even those from view.

It dwarfs us, dwarfs our entire station. Cold, black stone takes the heavens away entirely, and I step closer, peering up, desperate for any glimpse of starlight. A tiny sliver of space lingers, barely visible.

But Francois tugs at my hand, pulling me away from the little window.

"We need to buckle in," he says, frantic voice made tinny by the comm equipment spitting his words into my helmet. "Please, Jenna. We have to buckle in."

I let him drag me back to the wall, release his hand as he secures his harness. But I can only fumble with my own straps and buckles. My eyes never leave the window, never stop tracing the craggy asteroid, roaming over ravines and pockmarks.

A soft click rings out as I finish with the last buckle, latching myself to this death trap. As Francois wraps his hand around mine once more, I think of home.

I can still see my little house, still hear the sound of other people's ships off-planet leaving me behind. I still see Francois, smiling as he figured calculations at the desk across from me. I still feel the heat that built within me every time his strange golden eyes alighted on me, still feel the touch of his lips the first time he kissed me, just days before we left Earth.

I swallow hard as the asteroid moves closer, grey and black stone becoming crystal clear beyond the window. But I don't want that to be my last sight. I want to turn and look at Francois, want to stare into his golden eyes as it hits.

But my suit and harness hold me still.

A tear slides over my cheek, and I close my eyes. "Francois…" I say, voice thick. "I love you."

I've never spoken the words aloud before, never dared.

But he says, "I love you, too." Gravel roughs up the edges of his voice.

Choking back a sob, I grip his hand tighter.

And the asteroid hits our station.

Metal shrieks, groaning as its torn and smashed, and my heart lurches. Air rushes out through holes in the station walls, and alarms scream. I grip my armrest, dig my fingers into Francois' hand. Biting back sobs, I try to push the panic away.

But my Link reads off a steady scroll of sectors that have taken damage, cycling through every single one.

And the asteroid knocks us back, pushing us away from Terata.

Our boosters kick in, jolting us all in a desperate attempt to keep us in orbit. They use the last of our fuel, burning through it quickly, and I can't tell if they've done any good.

We seem to slow, and I open my eyes to find the wall moved in, the cracked window a mere meter from my face. Tears blur my vision, but I see the asteroid before us, the rest of the station wrapped around it like a death shroud. Bodies float near one of the sectors amidst droplets of blood, frozen and shining in the wan sunlight.

I choke back another sob, but Francois cries openly. The sound of it, echoing through my helmet sends a lance of pain through my heart.

"This is it," I say, realizing that the end is most certainly here. A sob racks my body, ragged and broken.

There's no one close enough to save us. The first ship of settlers won't even leave earth for a month. The other settlements are a two-week journey away.

How far will we drift in that time?

Will they even find our bodies?

Will they even look?

I shake my head. Even moving as slowly as we are, we'll drift away long before anyone gets here.

Already, the blood crystals and bodies are small. Just little white dots in red clouds. Only the asteroid and the twisted hunk of metal that was once our station are clear.

A strange, numb sort of peace falls over me, and I set my jaw.

I undo my harness one-handed, refusing to let go of Francois. "Come on," I say. "We have to be there. They have to be able to find us."

He unbuckles, and we squeeze past bent bulkheads and hoses emptying themselves of air. A massive hole gapes at the end of our sector, and we move toward it. It grows, looming, waiting to swallow us.

But the stars shine in the darkness, open arms waiting to welcome us.

Francois grips the edge of our sector, and I swing out into space, wrapping around to grab hold of a bent beam, sticking out near the window that showed us the asteroid.

"I have a good grip," I say. "You can let go."

And he does.

Floating around to me, he bends his arm, reeling himself in.

I glance over my shoulder at the asteroid, at the remnants of our station. Then, I meet his gaze, golden eyes shining beneath thick black lashes.

"Ready?" he asks.

I nod, and we position ourselves. Softly, we kick off, floating toward the asteroid. My stomach flips, and panic flutters through me. We wrap around each other, arms and legs twining together.

But it doesn't truly matter if we aimed properly.

We won't survive this, either way.

"Jenna…" he croaks.

And I hear it in his voice, the same hopelessness that grows within me, the same dark pit swallowing me up.

I nod once more.

Looking up, I watch the asteroid, searching for a point to grab it. We bump into it, and I scramble for purchase. My heart leaps into my throat as my hand slides over the surface, but I find a pit, a little pocket carved out of the side by some hapless object long ago.

Taking a deep breath, I stare into Francois' eyes.

"We should just float here now, if you want to let go," he says. "But... I don't want to just..." His voice falters. "I don't want to... wait."

"Me either," I whisper.

Surrounded by the wreckage of our home away from Earth, I keep my eyes on him as the crystalline blood cloud of one of our friends drifts by.

"On three?"

He opens his mouth to answer, but no words come out. He nods.

"Close your eyes, though. I don't want you to... I don't want you to see me after..." Tears fall over my cheeks, and my throat grows thick, cutting off my words.

"Jenna, I love you," he whispers. "I want to see you."

"Please, don't. I don't want you to see me frozen and—" A sob chokes the rest of my words.

He puts a hand to the side of my helmet, pulling me closer. The glass plates clink together, and he stares deep into my eyes.

I stare back, memorizing his sharp jaw, the dark stubble. I trace his short hair, gaze at the little flecks of brown buried within his golden irises.

He nods, one last time, then closes his eyes.

And then, I close mine.

"One," I say, voice hoarse.

"Two," he whispers, moving his hand from my helmet and wrapping his arm around my waist.

I pull him closer, wrapping both my arms around his neck. "Three."

With a thought, I tell my Link to lower my helmet. It wooshes back, and I brace myself for the cold I know will come.

But it doesn't.

Tears fall freely, and I wonder for a moment if I just didn't feel it, if I'm in the afterlife. I open my eyes to find Francois floating within my arms, silently sobbing. I touch his face, bewildered, and he looks at me.

He shakes his head, mouths, "What is this?"

I tear my eyes from him, gazing at the pale-grey ball that encapsulates us. My brows furrow, and my brain grapples with my surroundings, trying to make some sense of reality.

Impossibly, a section slides away, revealing a larger dome beyond. And a tall creature floats through.

Four arms, grey skin. It stares at us without emotion, green irises shifting and spinning. A fan of blue light bursts from its eyes, and I jump. The fan of light sweeps over us, and the alien says, "Prepare yourselves for gravity."

We fall, dropping to the bottom of the sphere with a thud. The creature with the see-through skull stares down at us, landing gracefully.

The wall of the sphere opens further, admitting two more aliens. They stare down at us, impassive. Moving slowly, methodically, they approach. Their moves are too precise, too even. It stands the hair up on the back of my neck.

"What's happening?" Francois asks.

"We know how humans fare in space. We learn nothing from your death," the alien says, voice flat. Only now do I realize it speaks our language.

Cold dread seeps through me.

"However," it goes on, monotone, face expressionless. "There is much we can learn from the remainder of your lives."

The Last Settlers

By Elexis Bell

Second prequel to The Regonia Chronicles

Author's Note:

The main series has a playlist written into it. That isn't the case for this prequel, with only one song mentioned in the story, so here are some of the main songs that I listened to while writing it, just in case you want to listen to them.

Sweet Savior by Villagers
Woman by Emmit Fenn
Last Rites by Dark Arts

Chapter One

Jordan

Shuffling forward, I stare through the window at the Cutlass, a massive spaceship, a behemoth of gleaming metal and high-tech engineering. It perches on the runway, itching to lift off. Beyond it, decrepit buildings hunch in the dust clouds that are slowly claiming Earth.

The boarding line moves forward, drawing my gaze inside once more. I take a few steps, hating how tightly my cryo-suit fits and longing for my own clothes. They rest aboard the ship though, packed for the trip through space.

My stomach turns at the thought of leaving Earth, of leaving my father, not that there's much choice.

If you're lucky enough to be chosen by the Survival Coalition for relocation to Termana, you thank whatever God you pray to and pack your shit.

You were chosen. It's a good thing.

A spray of pebbles batters the window as a dust devil whips by, battering the landscape for a few moments before tuckering itself out. A few scraggly plants claw their roots into the ground, scraping some sort of existence from what's left of the world. Their leaves wither in the heat, and they struggle to feed themselves in the hazy atmosphere.

A blurry mess of jagged outlines hide on the horizon, barely visible through the dust. The skyscrapers which make up downtown Houston are nothing more than menacing shadows, shifting like a desert mirage.

Engineers mill about the ship, checking and rechecking everything. Beads of sweat roll down their faces, leaving clean tracks in the dirt caked around their respirators and goggles. The air stains their white uniforms a yellow-brown. Sweat drenches their clothes, and that'll only get worse as morning rolls on toward afternoon.

My shoulders sag beneath the weight of memories toiling in Midwestern fields to keep the family farm running, struggling to feed the masses as the aftermath of supervolcano eruptions hung in the air. The stench of my respirator's sweat-soaked straps lingers in my nose, even after weeks of testing inside the Coalition's labs.

The image of my father lying in a hospital bed flashes through my mind, and my heart twists. I can still see the tube running to his nose, feeding oxygen into lungs too damaged to manage breathing on their own thanks to his stubborn refusal to wear a respirator outside.

And suddenly, I'm right back there again, making a joke to disguise the fear and bone-deep ache in my gut at the sight of him. "So, this is what it took to get you to wear a respirator?"

The nurse tries her best to hide her laugh, then grows serious as my father asks, "Why are you here?"

I stop in my tracks, hand clutching my drink as I stare at him. My head tips to the side.

"If you strand yourself on this dead rock just to watch me die, I'll know you're just in it for the inheritance," he says.

But I still stare at him, shocked.

The inheritance? The family farm that's been more and more useless with every passing year?

"Go," he says. "I'll not accept visitors anymore. Not if it means you condemn yourself to *this*." He gestures to the window, the landscape beyond made more bleak by his limp movement.

My shoulders fall, and tears slip from my eyes. But after a few more words and a sobbing embrace, chest collapsing and eyes burning, I agree to leave for Termana.

Blinking rapidly, the present slams back into me, a mess of blurred shapes thanks to the sheen of tears hovering on my lashes. I try to think of what Termana will be like, what my new life will be like.

But all I can think of is what the rest of *his* life will be like.

A month left to live...

He'll be gone before I wake up.

The thought slithers through me, rocking me to my core, and it takes everything I can to stay put, to keep myself in line rather than run back to Missouri, back to the hospital. But he wouldn't see me if I did, wouldn't permit my presence.

I clear my throat, pull in a deep breath. Wiping my eyes, I focus on the sterile white tiles at my feet, on the way my arms dangle uselessly at my sides, wrapped in the strange cryo-suit that feels a little bit like a freezer bag for food.

The woman in front of me takes a few steps, and I follow along, feet dragging me forward. A tall man asks her name, thankfully in the common tongue. The cochlear implant newly buried within my flesh still doesn't feel right when it speaks translations in that computerized voice.

"Kira Romero," the woman answers, voice as monotone as I feel. She touches her left forearm, feeling the place where her Link has been installed, the same as mine. Her fingers trace the rectangle of the screen through her cryo-suit.

She and the Coalition representative go back and forth confirming various information. Age: 28. Height: 5'7". Weight: 160 lbs.

That number strikes me as odd, given how slender the woman is.

Must be pretty strong.

When she confirms her occupation as a metal worker and welder, it makes sense. The tall man scans her retinas and checks her fingerprints, and she's allowed to move along.

Then, it's my turn.

I confirm myself to be a 30 year old, 6'0" tall, 180 lb farmer, then pass all identity checks and move forward through the terminal.

A short woman bustles about. Her respirator hangs lazily about her neck, having merely been pulled down when she came in for the day. Her short brown hair bounces against her scalp as she approaches.

"The two of you," she says, gesturing to Kira and me. "Stay together."

Before I can ask why, she's on to the people behind me, pairing them up. Not that she leaves me to wonder for long. Through the magic of the Link and the cochlear implant, when she speaks, even from twenty yards away, her voice rings in my head. "Those of you whom I've paired up, please, stay together. Your cryo-beds are situated together in the ship."

Kira and I glance at each other, and she gives me the shell of a smile. Eyes the color of warm molasses shine with fear, echoing the writhing mass of chaos slowly solidifying into a knot in my gut.

Sure, everyone wants to go to Termana, to be spared the relentless heat of our oven of a planet, to have some hope of a real future. But now, on the threshold of the Cutlass, the thought of leaving Earth seems alien. Saying goodbye to every place I've ever known, with the knowledge that my dad will be dead before I even wake up, makes panic well up within me.

A long sigh lifts Kira's chest, and she reaches out to me, wrapping her hand around mine. Our fingers lace together, and I squeeze her hand, glad for the comforting touch. My eyes drift down to our interwoven fingers.

Our nails gleam, absent of any grease or dirt beneath their edges, free of the persistent stains of a lifetime of manual labor. It's the cleanest my hands have been in as long as I can remember, and given her job, I assume the same is true for Kira. My eyes trace the multitude of scars marring her tan skin. Callouses adorn her fingers and the palms of her hands, much like my own.

And somehow, it's a relief, a little piece of something familiar as everything else falls apart.

The short woman moves through the ranks, bustling back to the front of the line, then leading us through the terminal toward the bridge attached to the ship. Neither Kira nor I pull apart, hands linked all the way through barren halls.

Hollow thuds ring out as the feet of those in front of us cross from the solid floor to a metal floor. I swallow hard as Kira and I step into the metal tube, moving slowly into a cargo bay that stretches the entire length of the Cutlass.

A single aisle divides the cavernous space. On either side, pairs of cryo-beds shaped, rather unfortunately, like coffins line the room. A tank of vivid blue liquid perches between the paired beds, attached to them with a slew of hoses.

The line moves forward, painfully slowly, and I scan each bed, looking at the names printed on their sides. One step forward brings me even with a new set of beds.

When we reach beds whose names begin with the letter P, I pay more attention. Porter consumes four beds, an entire row on either side of me, and I assume it belongs to a family. In the next set, a man named Jason Purcell is slotted to spend the next few months in a bed connected to a woman named Temperance Quinlan on my left, with the set on my right occupied by Juan and Miranda Ramirez.

In the next row, the cryo-beds to the right, the little metal boxes, bear our names.

Stepping free of the aisle and moving to stand between our cryo-beds, we stare down at the things which will be our homes for the coming months. The ship walls, once distant, seem to move inward, and the echoes of voices around me bounce off them. The cargo bay closes in, growing cramped and claustrophobic.

This is it.

I swallow hard.

I expected something more impressive than a sardine can.

The thick metal and heavy glass lid shine in the glaring lights of the cargo bay. Shadows play in the engraving of my name. The fingers of my right hand reach out, tracing the letters, clinging to the one thing which ties me to my past, to this place.

To my father.

A sharp intake of breath draws my gaze upward. Kira's syrup eyes overflow with tears, and her breathing grows shallower and faster by the minute.

A voice rings in my head, transmitted by the cochlear implant. In the common tongue, the woman from before says, "Please, step into your assigned cryo-beds."

Hundreds of hydraulics hiss through the cargo bay, and the lids of every single bed lift, then slide outward to allow entry. I jump at the deafening noise, and Kira's breathing accelerates. Releasing her hand, I step in front of her. I grasp her upper arms, and the black plastic of her cryo-suit crinkles.

"Hey," I whisper. "Look at me."

Wild and frightened, her eyes focus on mine for an instant, then dart around the room again, only to land on her cryo-bed.

In my ear, the same woman says, "Rodriguez, Romero. Please step into your beds."

"Not yet," I think, knowing my reply will reach her. The Coalition's tech may be far beyond what I thought we'd accomplished, bordering on un-believable, but it comes in handy. "Give us a minute."

Aloud, I say, "Kira, hey, look at me, please."

At long last, she does. Pupils dilated, her chest heaves as she hyperventilates. She reaches up, grasping my forearms.

"Breathe, okay? Just focus on your breathing."

I take a deep, slow breath to demonstrate, urging her to follow suit. She tries, but her lungs chop the breath into pieces. She shakes her head feebly, clutching my forearms tighter.

"That's good," I say. "Just keep breathing."

Several more intentionally drawn out breaths pass my lips. Her gaze is fierce, boring into my soul as she struggles to gain control of her body. All around us, people clamor into their cryo-beds, some staring over their shoulders to gawk at the panic sweeping through Kira, someone craning their necks to gawp at a similarly afflicted man at the front of the ship. Long minutes pass before any sort of pattern emerges within her lungs, but it does happen eventually.

"We've got this," I say. "*You've* got this. You can handle it. You're strong."

"You don't—" her breath hitches, "—even know me."

"Maybe not," I allow. "But you wouldn't be here if they thought you couldn't hack it."

Her grip loosens on my arms, and her fingers tremble against my cryo-suit. She closes her eyes, fanning long lashes against tan skin. Full lips purse with a deliberately slow breath.

Then, another.

And another.

When her eyes open once more, she nods. Fully in control of herself, except for the lingering catches in her lungs and the slight trembling in her fingers, she clears her throat, then says, "Thank you."

Knowing it will be my last chance at any human contact for many months, I pull her into my arms, wrapping her in an embrace. Her arms wind around my neck, and she takes several deep breaths.

Pulling back, faces inches apart, I fight the urge to kiss her, chalking it up to misplaced adrenaline. We nod, then separate.

Stepping into my cryo-bed, I remind myself that I won't notice the time spent in these cramped confines. When I wake, I won't feel as though I've gone almost half a year without any physical contact.

But as I lie down, I feel better going forward having felt warm arms around me.

The lid of my bed hisses to life as the hydraulics slide it into place over me, then lower it into the closed position. A few bolts slam into place, locking me in, and again, panic trickles down my spine. My heart gallops.

A sweet smelling gas puffs into the enclosed box, and I stare at the cargo bay ceiling through the glass lid. Shivers roll through me as the temperature plummets. My breath comes in clouds, fogging up the glass, and my eyes focus on that instead, my world shrinking to this box, this tiny existence. Bright blue liquid pours in through the hose attachment points near my shoulder and hip, frigid as it hits me.

Another puff of sweet gas filters in, and as I breathe it, my muscles relax. The thick liquid gushes in. My drugged mind tells me it's bright, blueberry jelly, and a small laugh crosses my lips.

My eyes fall shut as the coolant covers my fingers. The sloshing reverberates in my mind, echoing to fill the space left in the wake of meaningful thought. The liquid creeps up my scalp, trickling into my ear canals.

Thank God I shave my head.

A giggle flows through me as my body surrenders to the sedative and the cold.

My beard is going to be a mess.

Kira's long, brown ponytail floats through my thoughts, and I mumble, "Her hair is going to be gross after this..."

And then, cryo-sleep sneaks in to steal the months away.

Chapter Two

Kira

I move unsteadily through my new apartment, staring at the crates someone brought up while I thawed out. Stacked in my living room floor, they perch among the few pieces of furniture I was allowed to bring from home. My bed, my couch, and my dining set are all stacked in the corner.

A few workers mill about, moving things where I direct them, and I cringe at this dependence, this need for someone else to do such a basic thing as carry my box of clothes to my bedroom for me. But the lethargy and weakness left behind by cryo-sleep have rendered even such a simple task beyond me, forcing me to rely on others, something that's never really worked out well in the past.

My mind fills with the parents who gave me up as a baby, the negligent *caregivers* at the children's home, and the many jobs I worked through high school, saving money to escape that place. Working from the age of fourteen, I always knew the only person I could count on to keep my head above water was myself.

Looking around, I wonder if I should thank the unenthusiastic school counselor who didn't bother trying to discourage me from taking shop class. It gave me a direction to move in, luckily into a job that paid well enough to get me out on my own straight out of high school.

And got me here.

One of the workers drops the crate containing my bedding, and I sigh, rubbing a hand over my face. Retrieving a metal cup from the cabinet in my sterile, spartan kitchen, I fill it at the tap, all the while thanking my 'lucky' stars that there was nothing breakable in the crate he dropped.

My muscles ache as I settle onto a stool at the bar of the kitchen island. I turn sideways to lean back against the wall which leads to the front door, the wall which stretches the length of my living room and butts up against my neighbor's apartment.

Jordan Rodriguez.

The man with whom I walked onto, and off of, the Cutlass.

The memory of his arms sliding around me the second we stepped free of our cryo-beds settles over me, filling me with warmth. Still covered in the thick coolant, dripping globs of it everywhere, we clung to each other, chasing away the chill of cryo-sleep that had us both shivering.

I smile remembering his hand in mine the whole way through our check in, only parting when doctors made us, escorting us to separate rooms for showers and atrophy assessments. With that behind us, our hands found each other again each time.

Was that weird?

I tip my head to the side, considering it. But none of the doctors or Coalition representatives seemed surprised, and many of the others from the ship acted similarly.

My mind fills with the family that walked behind us onto the ship and ahead of us coming off it. The children were carried, the parents reaching out for each other with their free hands as if reassuring themselves that they weren't alone.

Not that cryo-sleep was all that traumatic, in and of itself. No nightmares haunted that sleep. No monsters lurked in the darkness of our minds, waiting to claim our bodies while the rightful owners were away on a five month vacation hurtling through space at 120,000 kilometers an hour.

But the thawing process brought with it the bone-deep knowledge that something unnatural just happened. The certainty, yet uncertainty, of waking months after falling asleep somewhere other than Earth.

And that, and only that, is why I reached out to Jordan.

A soft, blue glow emanates from my Link, pulsing, reminding me that I have video transmissions from Sheldon. But from when?

How many did he send while I was frozen?

Did he meet someone new, or decide not to come to Termana, after all?

I raise my brows at the stupidity of such a decision, but that doesn't exactly remove it from Shel's wheelhouse.

Taking a deep breath, I decide to wait, cringing inwardly at the idea of watching them with the movers bustling about my apartment. Heaven knows what Shel will say, or do, in the videos. Rubbing my temples, I groan.

Why am I even with him?

A million assessments of my own self-worth, or lack thereof, come flooding through me, and I shove them all away.

***

Perched on my couch, staring blankly at the barren wall, I close my eyes. Tugging the blanket tighter around myself, I nestle in, trying to chase a persistent chill from my bones. I breathe deeply for several seconds before opening them, finally ready, sort-of, to watch the first of Sheldon's messages.

Glancing at my Link, I think the commands, still unsettled by the tech's connection to my mind and body. The screen shows me Sheldon's apartment back on Earth as seen from his webcam.

"God, I hope I get used to this thing," I whisper.

A silent wish for a bigger picture, uttered only in my thoughts, prompts the wall across from me to blink to life like a screen.

"What...is happening?" I wonder aloud, stunned.

But it must be a screen embedded in the wall because the video transmission from Sheldon begins to play upon it.

His apartment, which I cleaned before I left knowing he wouldn't do it for a long while, is dingy. Clothes drape over the back of his dark, brown couch, and dishes sit in tall, haphazard stacks in the sink behind it. A few lights glow throughout the place, a necessity given the dust caked to the outside of all the windows, blocking out the sun. Sheldon comes over, and plops down on the couch, hair and clothes unwashed.

Must be a day off work.

I check the date of the transmission.

Only five days, and he's already made a mess of his apartment and himself.

Wait. It took him five days to send me a message?

I expected two, maybe three, since he was about to work two long days. But five days?

My insides twist.

"So, that's what I mean to him?"

Our dysfunctional relationship plays out in my mind, lingering on the arguments over whether I should do more for him than I already do and whether I should tolerate so many slip-ups.

His voice booms out through speakers tucked into the walls throughout the living room. "Kira," he says, almost sweetly, but the sentimental tone is ruined by the way his words vibrate my bones.

"Holy shit, that's loud, I exclaim, covering my ears.

The volume adjusts automatically.

Maybe I can get used to this thing in my arm, after all.

"This sucks," Shel says. "I guess I miss you. It's weird, not having you around."

My brows come together as he scratches his temple restlessly, and his dark eyes fall to the ground. Pursing his full lips, he slumps back into the couch, letting it cradle him.

"I go in for more tests next week and then more a couple weeks after that. All a formality, of course. They're going to choose me," he says, ever confident. Or maybe it's cockiness after a certain point. "After that, I'll know how long until I can come up there. Down there. Out there? Whatever direction it is, I'll know when I can head your way. I guess I'll let you know, then. Be good up there, Kira."

The wall goes blank with the end of his transmission, and a strange emptiness settles in my stomach. I try not to think about the two work days or the three days off work that he didn't care enough to send me a message. I try not to think of how it's merely *weird* to him that I'm not around.

A knock at the door jars me out of my thoughts, and I rise from the couch, tossing my blanket down upon it. As I meander past the kitchen and down the hall to the door, rubbing my hands up and down my arms to warm up, the image on the wall disappears, retreating to the depths of my Link once more.

I open the door to find Jordan smiling down at me. My stomach flutters, such an odd sensation. Such a rare sight on Earth, maybe impossible here, and yet a whole flock of butterflies seems to have taken up residence within me. Each second staring into his smoldering, grey eyes wakes another, warming its tiny body so that it might flap its wings, beating them against my heart.

But I don't trust the sensation, *can't* trust it.

Clearly, my taste in men leaves something to be desired.

"Want to go get some food with me?" he asks.

The warmth in his voice pushes me past my reservations. I nod, thankful that he's come to spare me having to watch the rest of Sheldon's videos for the time being. He reaches out his hand, and though I hesitate, I take it. A bit of the chill that's followed me since we woke up here recedes.

Pressed against my wrist, his Link pulses with the same soft, blue glow as mine.

Who's he avoiding?

Chapter Three

Jordan

We descend the stairs to the lobby of our apartment building, the metal ringing hollowly underfoot. Kira squeezes my hand, sending a trill of warmth through me. Glass doors, or maybe plastic, something clear in any case, show us the faux world beyond. I startle at the visibility, at the lack of dust coating them in a filmy layer.

And the world beyond is no less strange.

A street lined with metal box buildings, each with a tiny plot of lively green plants out front, the likes of which we haven't seen on Earth in... years. Not outside of a greenhouse, anyway.

The door swings open for us, and we step outside. I breathe the air, fill my lungs to bursting, and Kira does the same. Out of habit, my free hand reaches to adjust the strap of my respirator, and though I feel the ghost of it, feel the phantom pressure of its straps wrapped around my head, my fingers touch only my shaved scalp. Instantly, I think to tell Dad, to message him and say that I'm outside without a respirator for the first time in years, that I can breathe.

But he's already gone.

My heart lurches, and I slow to a stop. My head fills with what his last days must've been like, alone in that hospital bed, withering away until the pain grew so great that they kept him unconscious.

I close my eyes, swallowing hard. The soft, blue pulse of my Link glows, slipping through the cracks of my eyelids to remind me that he sent me messages. Or maybe I simply imagine the pale glow at the edges of my lids, maybe it's entirely blocked.

Kira steps closer, even as she pulls her hand from mine and slips her arm around my waist. Putting my own around her shoulders, I tug her against me, burying my face in her hair as we settle into the embrace. I cling to her, desperate for something solid and real and warm.

I hope she wouldn't call me a terrible person for abandoning my father to die alone.

***

We sit on a small couch in a cafe after a slew of flirtatious advances from the barista, and the woman's face falls as Kira and I curl toward each other, sipping our warm drinks. My coffee goes down smooth, artificial though it may be until they get another greenhouse working that maintains the right conditions for coffee beans.

Kira leans into my side, her head on my shoulder. My free arm drapes around her. She doesn't ask about the messages I haven't checked yet, and I don't ask about hers. She doesn't pry about the people I left behind, and I don't ask about those she left on Earth.

We only sit, sipping and wondering what life will be like here. When the barista brings the sandwiches we ordered out to us, we separate, but only out of necessity. The moment we've both eaten, our hands twine together once more.

***

At the door to her apartment, she hesitates before going in. I search her gaze, and she swallows once. Stepping forward, I touch her neck and lean in. My lips brush hers, and though her hands grip my waist, holding tight, she doesn't return the kiss.

I pull away, just far enough for her lips to move against mine as she whispers, "I... I have a boyfriend. Back on Earth. He might be coming here."

34

Sighing, I let my forehead rest against hers. I don't mention the odds of him being selected. I only say, "Okay. Still friends?"

Not that there's been much of a friendship to ruin, but she feels like the only real connection I have. Sure, we've only known each other for a couple days. The day we went onto the ship, the day we came off it, and now today. Unless you count the months spent next to her in cryo-sleep.

But she feels more real than the friends who essentially cut me out of their lives after learning of my selection for relocation.

She nods, hands still on me, fingers digging into my waist in a way that heats my blood. Her eyes dart to her door. "Since we're friends… Do you want to hang out? Maybe play a game or watch a movie or something? I just… I don't really want to sit in there alone all night."

A single look at my own door, the notion of sitting with my thoughts and the messages I still haven't watched, the news of my father's death that I'm sure they hold, nearly knocks the air from my lungs.

So, I nod, then let her lead me into her apartment. A few boxes linger in the corner of the living room, not much different than my own place. The whole apartment seems to be a replica of mine, every room laid out the same.

Her hand comes to rest on the small of my back as I pass her, and she closes the door. My eyes dart to the hall I know must lead to her bedroom, and I swallow hard.

She has a boyfriend.

He's on Earth.

He might never get here, but she still has a boyfriend.

Breathing deeply, I venture toward the pale, grey couch. She moves through the kitchen, filling two glasses of water.

"You can sit down," she says. "You don't have to wait for me."

I nod, eyeing the couch that seems even smaller now that I'm closer. Two cushions, neither very large, wait for us. I settle in, arm draped along the back of the couch out of habit. As she approaches, I think better of it, bringing it to rest on my lap.

"So, what do you want to watch?" I ask.

"I don't know," she says, cheeks coloring a bit. "Usually if I was watching something with someone, Shel would insist on Basketball."

"Well, I guess that's good to know and all, but what do *you* want to watch?" I say. I stop myself from commenting on the fact that he isn't here to insist on anything.

"Promise you won't judge me? And we don't have to watch it if you don't want to," she says, placing both glasses on a little wooden table.

I smile, keeping my eyes carefully above her toned physique to hold her gaze. "I won't judge. What is it?"

She drops down onto the couch beside me, thigh brushing mine and shoulder pressed against me. Butterflies flit about in my stomach, and I forget the thread of our conversation, forget that I could ever judge her harshly.

"There was this really old cooking show where they did a lot of baking back on Earth. It was a competition, but they were just so nice to each other," she says. "It's super low drama, really relaxing."

My smile widens because I think I know exactly what show she's talking about.

But she shrinks. "You said you wouldn't judge."

My shoulders fall, and my brows come together. I consider her and wonder if maybe her wonderful boyfriend made fun of her for this or something.

"I'm not," I assure her. "I smiled because I know the show. My mom used to love it. My dad started watching it more after she was gone."

She relaxes again, face softening. With a nod and apparently a command through her Link, the screen before us illuminates, showing us a world of pastries that neither of us will ever know.

She settles in, leaning back and drawing her legs up beneath her. Our shoulders press together, and her knees rest atop my thigh. The bakers go about their business, making dough and being nice to each other.

The couch seems to swallow me up, pulling me deeper into its cushions. Lingering tendrils of exhaustion from thawing out yesterday simply further the effect.

Kira melts beside me, leaning against my side, and I lift my arm to wrap it around her shoulders. As we watch the pleasantries of a world so far from us, far even from the world of dust and death we left behind, the bone-deep loneliness of cryo-sleep rises up within me once more.

Until her arm slips around me, resting on my stomach, and her head settles on my shoulder.

Warmth flows through me, and sleep tugs at my eyelids.

Chapter Four

Kira

Blinking drowsily, I draw in a deep breath. Jordan's arms hold me close, and I sit nestled against him on the couch. He still sleeps, breath coming deep and even. His warmth flows through my veins, but guilt chases it.

Swallowing hard, I wonder at the time, and my Link speaks softly into my mind.

3:12 a.m.

Sitting up, I move carefully so as not to wake Jordan. My hand slides from his stomach, and his arms drop from around me. One hits the couch. The other lands on his lap, and he startles awake. His golden eyes snap open, and he searches the room, gaze landing on me. He smiles, a soft, drowsy smile, and heat pools within me.

Again, guilt burns me.

"You okay?" he asks.

I nod and whisper, "Bathroom."

"Why are you whispering? Afraid you'll wake your neighbor?" he asks, lips turning up in a wry grin.

Laughing, I shake my head. "Looks like I already did that. Be right back."

His laugh makes my stomach flip, but that isn't the only reason my cheeks burn. I rise to my feet, dragging myself to the bathroom and hoping I don't look as ashamed as I feel.

I shouldn't be curling up next to him, friends or not.

Shel will be here soon.

Well, not soon, but that doesn't matter.

I slide the bathroom door open, stepping inside without looking back. It closes silently, and I lean back against it. My hands rise to cover my face as I try to drown out the little voice in the back of my head that won't stop whispering that Shel is self-obsessed, that he's no good, that he treats me more like a maid than a girlfriend.

It doesn't matter.

He's my boyfriend, and I can't do this to him.

Lifting my arm, I prompt my Link to play the next message from Sheldon. Fear that Jordan may hear immediately translates through the Link, and it plays the audio through my cochlear implant.

On the tiny screen in my wrist, Sheldon appears, running a hand through hair gone shaggy without me there to set up appointments for haircuts. But there's less clutter on the counters in the kitchen, fewer dishes on the table before him. His collar bones peek out through a smattering of hair on his bare chest.

He begins to speak, mouth opening, but it closes quickly as he turns to look over his shoulder. In the doorway to his bedroom, a woman appears, clad in one of his t-shirts. It drapes over her figure, reaching down to bare thighs.

My stomach sinks.

He's sleeping with someone else?

Is this a break up message?

He says something to the woman, but I don't hear it over the rushing in my ears. All I see is her pretty smile, her tousled hair falling around her shoulders, the way she leans against the door frame, hand wrapped around it and knee rising against it as she gives him a wicked look.

"I'll be there in a minute," he says, then turns back to the camera.

Shame burns my cheeks.

"That's what I wanted to talk to you about, Kira," he says. "Look, I hope you didn't expect me to wait. The soonest I'll get up there to you is eight months. I have needs."

My mouth goes dry, and my insides turn.

You could've waited more than a couple weeks.

Cold realization sweeps through me. He messaged after five days. Then, couldn't be bothered for a couple weeks.

"I'm sure you have needs, too. Do what you need to up there," he goes on to say. "Just don't get yourself knocked up before I get there."

I stare at the little screen, appalled at what he's done and ashamed of myself for falling asleep next to Jordan, for not pushing him away the second he kissed me earlier. I may not have kissed him back, but it still feels like a betrayal.

But what does it matter if this is what Sheldon did with his time?

On the screen, he sits forward. "Well, that was pretty much it. Be good up there."

He reaches for the camera, and the message ends.

I swallow hard, hating the turn this has taken. My heart twists, and my stomach flops. And then, another thought draws my brows together.

He said not to get myself knocked up.

Does he not know they give everyone birth control for the first year?

Shouldn't they have mentioned that in his screening process by now?

I try to remember the order in which they did things, but it all blurs together in an amalgam of tests and needles and consultations. But I think they talked about that pretty early.

Are they not sending him?

Relief flows through me, but that shouldn't be what I feel. I should be upset or mad.

But the only anger I feel is for him.

And all I can see is that woman in his doorway.

Is she the reason the place was less of a wreck?

I stare at the bathroom around me, at the cold, sleek shower, the smooth sink. But I don't really see it, only blurs shaped roughly like a bathroom. A chill moves through me, settling in my gut. My Link glows a soft blue, reminding me that I still have messages to check, but I'm not sure I can stomach another, not right now.

Running my hands over my face, I turn away from the door. My hands find cold steel handles, and I turn on the tap, bending to splash water over my face. Little droplets fall from my nose, joining their brethren in a race down the drain, and light plays among them.

Reaching for the towel, I dry my face and stand, peering over the cloth still pressed to my mouth at the woman in the mirror. A million descriptors of myself, of how I am when I'm with Sheldon, come to mind, and I don't like a single one of them.

Docile. Caretaker. People-pleaser. Doormat.

It's like my backbone just melts around him.

Is that really the kind of woman I am?

But I know it is.

I kept up the charade of being happy with him through every interview during the screening. Maybe they wouldn't have let me come if they knew what I put up with, knew how weak I am.

But it's not like he's the worst.

He doesn't yell or hit me or anything.

He's just cocky and rude, sometimes. And a slob.

But he works so much, he's exhausted when he gets home. And he just doesn't have time to waste around with small talk and niceties.

I exhale loudly.

And I'm making excuses again, defending him, even to myself.

I meet my own eyes in the mirror, hands falling to clutch the towel to my chest. My lips move into a frown, and I almost apologize to my reflection.

And he's cheating.

My stomach drops. I close my eyes, breathing deeply.

A soft knock on the door makes me jump, and I press a hand to my chest.

"Kira?" Jordan asks. "Are you okay?"

I glance at my Link to find that somehow, I've managed to hide away in here for nearly twenty minutes. "Yeah," I say, voice quiet. Clearing my throat, I try again. "Yeah, sorry. I'll be out in a minute."

"Okay," he says, voice still edged with concern.

Drawing a fortifying breath, I hang the hand towel up and turn off the water. My hands fidget at the hem of my shirt, straightening it, then sweep my hair into a semblance of order. Finally, I head back out into the living room. Jordan sits on the couch, watching the bakers with a smile that softens when he turns his gaze to me. My heart flutters, and I sit next to him once more.

***

I wake with a crick in my neck and shift to ease it. A warm arm pulls me closer, wrapped around my shoulders, and another tightens around my waist. I open my eyes to find Jordan lying on his back, holding me on the couch. My head rests on his chest, and my hand lies centimeters from my face, fingers splayed across the hint of his collar bone that peeks out above the neck of his shirt.

He breathes deeply, chest rising beneath me, then turns slightly toward me. My leg rests between his, tangled up, and butterflies swarm in my stomach.

I almost pull away, almost sit up and get to my feet, but in my mind, I see the woman in Sheldon's bedroom door, half dressed and waiting for him. Eyes searching Jordan's peaceful features, I silently ask my Link the time. When it informs me that my alarm will sound in just three minutes, I let my head rest on Jordan's chest once more. My eyes close, and I try to make my peace with where I'm at.

Far away from Sheldon and a dying Earth.

One of the few who've been chosen to carry on and build Termana up, chosen to live.

Possibly soon to be single, if I can ever make my mind up about Sheldon.

But for the remaining minutes before my alarm, I resolve to focus only on Jordan's deep, even breaths.

***

My new supervisor, a man named Ikemba, leads me around the main workshop, explaining that only the most expensive, and thus the most precious, equipment is stored here. Most of it consists of large 3D printing machines and massive CNC machines that manufacture any replacement parts we may need.

"Repairs are mostly done on site," he says. He leans against a workbench, lanky frame towering over me but falling far shy of the height of the equipment around us. "Each main hub in the shell has an auxiliary workshop for welding or rewiring or, well, nearly anything. They're stocked with all the tools you could need, but there's a limited number of them. Lost tools have to be replaced with new ones made here. Broken tools have to be remade here too, so try not to shatter a wrench or anything."

My brows come together, and I stare at him.

I've never shattered a wrench.

He puts his hands up in a supplicating gesture, dark skin creasing as he smiles. "I know, I know. Not something that happens everyday. But you'd be surprised what I've seen up here. The stress of this place is different, especially working on the Shell. One wrong move, and we all die. It adds pressure to even the smallest jobs."

"That does up the ante, I suppose," I say, glancing up at the Shell far above us.

"That it does. With that said, and I assume they covered this back on Earth, but I'd rather be safe than sorry, there's a counselor in each apartment building. Feel free to set up appointments. Honestly, I'd recommend it, even if you feel okay, just to make sure you have an established counselor for just in case you start to struggle later. It's easier to maintain standing appointments than get up the nerve to go to a counselor when you're already struggling."

Surprise pulls my jaw low, and I swallow. They told us about the counselors in every apartment building, and on every block of houses where families reside, sure. They said that it would be free, a basic human right, especially since the consequences of leaving Earth and starting over in space and surviving while the planet dies, the long-term effects it could have on mental health, are still largely unknown.

I simply hadn't expected to hear it so highly endorsed by my boss.

I say, "Fair enough."

"You'll be on a regular schedule here, so setting up the appointments should be simpler that way. Just let me know if you need things moved around though," Ikemba says.

His warm smile is easy, and I cast my mind back over my previous bosses on Earth. Try as I might, I can't remember a single one that actually seemed to give a shit. When I say as much, he laughs.

From behind him, far back in the workshop, a woman with a shaved head wearing a t-shirt under her overalls calls, "He has to lock you in here. Lull you into a false sense of security." She laughs at her own comment, but so does he.

"Don't listen to Anaiah," he says, voice pitched loud even as he covers his mouth and leans in as if he were whispering.

"I heard that!" she says, rolling her eyes.

"Because you're not wearing your ear plugs," he calls back.

She settles her tools on the workbench before her and looks at him, exasperated. "Nothing's running. It's quiet."

He smiles, stepping up to a machine, pressing a few buttons. "Not anymore," he calls, then presses one final button. The CNC machine starts up, covering her laugh.

But she puts in her ear plugs, and so do we.

My smile creases my cheeks, and I wonder if every machine shop has this same sense of humor. The one back home certainly did.

Chapter Five

Jordan

"It isn't what our ancestors had, but it's as close as we can get," Aarya says.

She leads me through a field full of sprouts, green and beautiful. No spots adorn their leaves. No hints of disease from ash or pollution. No dry patches.

Clear air lets the overhead UV lights shine, unimpeded, upon the tiny plants. They're almost bright enough to block out the sight of the shell, though when I squint, I see that it's been painted a soft, light blue here to further the illusion.

Once again, I reach up as if to adjust the straps of my respirator, only to find it absent. Aarya catches me, and a smile decorates her face, creasing warm brown skin.

"Old habits die hard," she says. "I still do it every now and then, and I was on one of the first settler ships."

She bends to touch a leaf, and I look out over row after row of plants, all different kinds, all the plots in different stages of growth to ensure a constant supply of food. In the distance, the most mature plants bear fruits and vegetables of all kinds, and behind them, a vast expanse of golden wheat sways in the breeze of one of the largest fans I've ever seen.

I spin in place, taking it all in, and my eyes prick with unshed tears. My hands rise to rest atop my head, fingers twining together, as I stare in wonder.

I wish you could see this, Dad.

My Link pulses soft blue, reminding me that his messages are still there, and in some small way, it almost feels like he's here with me, still alive.

Every part of me wants to lie down between the rows of this field, to feel the breeze from that fan and breathe the clean air, to ditch my boots and let my toes sink into the dirt, artificially manufactured or not. It may not be the Earth of old, but it isn't the Earth as it is, either. My heart twists for the wreckage we made of our home, but we have a second chance here.

"It's a lot to take in," Aarya says. "And there's an adjustment period here too, as far as changing up how you do things. We don't have to battle the dust, and we don't have to compensate for soil turned too acidic by the crap that falls on it. The lights don't have to be cleaned as often as any set up on Earth. Watering is different too since this dirt holds it differently, though that's mostly automated by the drip hoses."

She goes on, and I do my best to listen. But if she's been here since the first settler ship, she's likely seen a slew of newbies struggle to come to terms with the beauty of this place. Something tells me she knows she'll have to repeat a few things.

***

Kira smiles at me as we settle in at her counter to eat. I shift on my stool, and she digs into the food she picked up on her way home from work. Her Link still glows the same blue as mine, casting light over her sandwich as she tells me about the work she'll be doing on the next sector.

"I'm not sure why I thought it was all done," she says. "I guess the main Shell is, but not all the sectors are ready for people to move in. It's airtight, but it still needs more bracing before all the life support can be hooked up."

I shake my head, surprised. "I thought it was all done. Didn't they say it was?"

She shrugs. "They might've said our *sectors* were done, but I'm not sure. A lot of it was a blur, just... tests and appointments and blood work and a ton of forms."

My lungs fill with a deep breath, and it leaves me slowly. Nodding, I nudge the chips on my plate with a finger.

The days of the selection process come back to me in a haze of trying to get to appointments and still get everything done on the farm, fitting in sleep and meals wherever I could, passing out in waiting rooms or in a chair in Dad's hospital room.

Then, everything changed when I was chosen. Abandoning the farm, handing it over to the neighbors. Barely getting time to visit Dad because I was packing or doing final fitness preparation for cryo-sleep. Sitting in more waiting rooms for birth control shots or going into surgery for the Link and the cochlear implant.

"They probably could've told us there were aliens living here, and I don't honestly know if I would've noticed," I say, voice hushed.

Kira laughs, but the sound is subdued. We eat in silence after that. My free hand itches to reach for hers. It rests mere centimeters from mine on the counter, as if she's debating the same thing.

She has a boyfriend.

"Were you always a farmer?" she asks, disrupting my thoughts.

I nod. "Runs in the family. Or it did." My tone turns somber, and my eyes dart to my Link.

"Sorry," Kira whispers. "If it helps, you're still in the family business."

I shake my head. "It's okay. And… that's not quite what I meant. My…" Voice breaking, I clear my throat and try again.

"My dad grew up before the respirators were mandated. So, even though we were deemed essential and given top of the line respirators by the Coalition after the mandates, he refused to wear his. Refused to go to the hospital, too," I say, voice growing thick as I recall the arguments, the staunch refusal, the stubbornness in his gaze as he told me time and again to take care of myself because he was a grown man, because his lungs were likely gone before the respirators.

"When he got too weak to get up, too weak to fight me on it, I loaded him up and took him to the hospital." The feeling of his frail body in my arms, far lighter than his tall frame should've been, assails me, and my chest heaves. "They said he had about a month. I almost didn't come here, almost stayed with him," I say, glancing at my wrist once more.

I can't look at Kira, can't watch her as she realizes that means he died while I slept.

Her hand wraps around mine, warmth flowing from her touch, and my eyes trace the shape of our hands. Tiny scars mar our skin, and though clearly strong, her hand looks small covering mine.

And boyfriend or not, I couldn't stop myself from closing my hand around the fingers wrapped under my palm even if I wanted to.

"Want some company while you watch the messages?" she offers in a whisper.

"You don't have to do that," I say, an automatic response.

Somehow though, it might be easier to hear his goodbye if I weren't alone.

"I know I don't have to. I asked if you want company. It's not the same thing," she says with a gentle smile.

Finally meeting her eyes, I smile back and say, "I might shatter my tough guy facade though."

"Tough guy is synonymous with emotionally and mentally stunted, in my mind."

Laughing, *somehow* laughing, I agree. Then, I dip my head toward her Link and ask, "Want company for yours?"

She shakes her head. "Shel is... not the best."

She makes an effort at hiding her emotions, and though I see it for the act it is, it's effective enough to keep me from parsing out whatever she holds back. I swallow hard, searching her gaze.

Teasing, I say, "So, he's 'not the best' and you still didn't kiss me back?"

She chuckles. "Just because he's not the best doesn't say anything about my character."

"Fair enough," I admit, using the hand she doesn't hold to lift a chip from my plate. "So why's he not the best?" I ask, then pop the chip into my mouth.

She chews at a bite of her food far longer than seems necessary, considering me, maybe considering her answer. Finally swallowing, she says, "He's arrogant. And a slob. Though it feels bad to say that since he's not here to defend himself. And those things kind-of come along with the whole doctor thing, I think."

"Arrogant, maybe," I allow, having only met one or two doctors in my life that weren't. "How does the slob thing come along with it though? I'd assume cleanliness would be important."

"Cleaning a whole apartment after an 18 hour shift sounds terrible," she says.

"I cleaned up after myself and my father after 16 hour shifts all summer long," I say. "It's easier if you don't make a mess to begin with. But I guess being a slob makes that part harder."

She rolls her eyes, smiling all the while, and heat flows through me. And though she squeezes my hand, my heart sinks when I glance at the soft blue glow of her Link.

***

Another farmer, a woman named Anettya, stands close as we sort seeds at a sturdy, metal table in a metal building near a field of engineered dirt. The surreal feeling of it all crashes over me, but she smiles warmly whenever our eyes meet. Her fingers brush mine as she takes a small plastic container of seeds from my hand, and she eyes me coyly.

Her dark hair sticks out of a short ponytail. Her jeans, a few sizes too large for her, hang loose, and though I can't imagine a reason she'd choose that, I don't ask, don't truly care. But when she catches me eyeing them, she must assume I looked for a different reason.

Settling the seeds aside on a shelf, she leans back against the table, hands braced upon it and ample chest stuck out. Her tank top clings to her slim waist, strains at her chest as she pulls in a deep breath.

"We have this pretty much done," she says, tipping her head toward the seeds. "And Aarya doesn't expect us at the field for another half hour."

She reaches for my hand, taking it in hers and pulling me forward. I stand before her, brows coming together as I wait for her to say more, debating on whether I should grab the seeds again or not.

Her other hand touches my waist, sliding up to my chest. "I can think of a few ways to spend that half hour," she says, standing up straight so that her chest presses against me.

I consider refusing her for a multitude of reasons.

We're at work. Someone could walk in.

Kira might find out.

But Kira wouldn't care. She has a boyfriend.

And as Annetya's lips find my neck, as her hands slip beneath the hem of my shirt, trailing along sensitive skin just above my waistband, the other reasons float away.

She kisses my neck, fingers gliding up over my stomach, then back down my ribs, and I let my eyes close, soaking in the feeling of a warm body against mine. The lingering chill of cryo-sleep fades into the furthest recesses of my mind as my hands rise to grip her hips, to pull her hard against me.

A soft sound of delight slips past her lips, warm breath gusting over my ear, and a shiver runs through me. She meets my gaze with a devilish grin, then brings her lips to mine. Our mouths meld, tongues dancing, and I push her against the table. She grinds her hips against mine, as if I had any doubts of her intentions, and heat races through me.

And though curling up with Kira, holding her on the couch, somehow sounds more appealing, though those moments of intimacy do a more thorough job of chasing the bone deep chill away, I find that the feel of Annetya's hands on the buttons of my pants and the gentle curve of her backside in my grasp does a fine enough job of it.

***

Annetya casts a wicked grin my way as she pulls her shirt back on. I button my jeans, breaths still coming quick, and return her smile.

"You'll be very popular," she says, pulling her pants up.

I furrow my brows, and she needs no more invitation to continue.

"You didn't know? Newbies are always popular, if they're... willing to participate. Not all of us want to start our families right away when we get here. We have to want families to come here, but that doesn't mean we want them within the first few years. The birth control only lasts a year, so for me... it's worn off."

She steps closer to me, hand sliding up my chest.

"Yours is still working hard," she whispers, leaning to kiss my neck. "And there are quite a few women willing to put it to work."

A shiver runs through me as her breath crashes over my neck.

Chapter Six

Kira

"It's official," Anaiah says. "Kristoff and Ikemba have released you from the shop. They're confident that you know your way around all the tools and machines here, which is obvious or you wouldn't be here, and that you aren't cracking up from cryo-sleep and leaving the world behind."

I yawn, putting a hand over my mouth, and laugh the second the yawn ends. "Sorry. That doesn't sound boring, I promise. I'm just slow to wake up, and the coffee is... weird."

She leans forward, bracing her arms on the workbench. "That's because it's not coffee, not really. It's some mushroom stuff. The greenhouse set to temperatures coffee plants like is reserved for other, supposedly more important, plants."

I smile, setting my cup of, apparently mushroom, coffee on my workbench. The drive motor I disassembled and remanned over the last couple days sits atop it, ready to go to storage since it met their standards when they checked it over last night.

"I'll put this up before we go," I say.

"That's what I like to hear." She grins, standing up straight and waiting patiently for me to stow the drive motor with the rest.

I grab my coffee, and she leads me through the shop. A quick ride on one of the strange, small public transport vehicles that run here takes us to a large metal wall that separates this sector from the next, and we walk to the bulkhead. I stare at it in wonder, marveling at the ingenuity and work that went into this place.

And I get to be a part of it.

Breathing deeply, filled with a sense of awe, I run my eyes over the junctions of I-beams, the countless rivets, the kilometers of conduit, and wonder how in the hell they ever built this place.

No wonder so much of the asteroid belt was cleaned up.

It's all right here, melted down and shaped to build all of this.

At the bulkhead, Anaiah scans her Link, and the door opens, allowing us access to a small vestibule. On either side, sleek, metal lockers line the walls. Labels denote their contents, and a few have scanners to limit access to the items within.

"Respirators are in the ones by the door," she says, walking ahead.

"Respirators?"

She nods, reaching into a square locker and retrieving one. She gestures to the locker next to it, and I dutifully retrieve a respirator. She puts hers on, and I follow suit.

"They're a precaution," she says, and her voice comes across my cochlear implant, crystal clear.

The mics of all the respirators back home always lent a tinny quality to anything said through them, but these are, like everything else here, state of the art. So when she goes on, I hear the tightness in her throat as emotion hangs on her words.

"A year ago, there was a..." She trails off, clears her throat. "A power surge fried the drives controlling the oxygen support in this sector. Obviously, we still don't have the backup in place, since that's what we're working on now, what *you'll* be working on later today after you get the tour. We definitely didn't have it up then."

A tear hovers on her lashes, and she swipes it away. Turning, she scans her Link at the door into the new sector. We step through, and the door closes.

"I was in there, working on some struts to hold the water treatment system," she says, growing quiet. "Kristoff was working with me, so was Carina. I don't think you've met her yet. We were… Well, not close to the airlock, but close enough."

Airlock.

I glance back at the vestibule falling further and further behind us and realize that's exactly what that was. A trill of fear trickles through me.

"We didn't make it to the airlock before we passed out, but we got close enough for medical to get to us in time," she says. "My sister, Marlina... She'd gone to get a tool from another workshop further in after ours broke. She… She didn't make it."

My heart stutters in my chest, and I mutter platitudes that I know can't possibly help.

Anaiah nods, then goes quiet for a while, walking along the road in this empty place. It branches out from the wall we passed through for a long way, far enough that I can't see it or the next wall. Empty buildings that'll eventually be homes or stores or offices sit on all sides, dark and though not sinister, eerily vacant.

This is the last thing that poor woman saw.

A shudder rolls through me.

"So, we wear respirators in here. Non-negotiable," Anaiah says.

I nod, happy to obey to that rule.

*****

I come down from the ladder, shaking out my arms. My shoulders burn from turning wrenches above my head for hours, but I look up at the platform we've built and breathe a little easier.

Metaphorically, anyway.

State of the art or not, I hadn't missed the feeling of having a respirator strapped to my face for hours on end.

But it's quitting time now, and though it took a long time, we finished the platform for the oxygen recyclers.

Kristoff, a large man with a ruddy complexion and shaggy dark hair going grey at the temples, pats me on the back. "Good work, kiddo."

I laugh, having never been called that in my life. "Kiddo?" I ask.

"What? You're a hell of a lot younger than I am. You look like a baby to me, like you should be in high school. No offense," he says. "Everyone under the age of thirty looks that way."

I laugh harder. "You can't be that much older than thirty. And I'm twenty-eight. Barely under thirty."

"I'm forty-five, thank you," he says, wiping his hands on his mech jumpsuit. "I've earned every one of those years, too."

I smile, not quite sure how he means that, but it doesn't matter. The warmth in his gaze puts me at ease.

"Watch out, Kira," another mechanic, a man by the name of Akimitsu, says. "He's going to Papa Bear you."

Grinning, I pull my gloves off, stuff them half into my back pocket. "He's going to what?"

"*Papa Bear* you," Akimitsu says. "First, he calls you a baby, then he treats you like one, then he acts like you're *his* baby. And his wife is just as bad."

"We only treated you like a baby because you acted like one," Kristoff says, but his smile never leaves his face.

"Hey, I had a broken finger. Leave me alone about that already." Akimitsu tosses his gloves onto a shelf, crossing his arms.

"And why did you have a broken finger?" Kristoff asks. He crosses his arms, mirroring the younger man, then widens his stance. With one arched brow, he waits.

"Because I didn't listen to you. I know, I know."

"Exactly. You were too stubborn and impatient to wait for my help and smashed your poor little baby finger, didn't you?"

I laugh, head falling back.

"Yeah, yeah," Akimitsu says, and a hint of color creeps onto his olive toned cheeks. Turning to me, he says, "This is what you're in for if you keep hanging out with him."

"Well, you see," I begin. "I wait for help if I need it, so..."

Kristoff bellows out a laugh, and Akimitsu shakes his head at us both.

Chapter Seven

Jordan

Kira and I settle in on her couch, and my face flushes with guilt. I run a hand over my beard, still damp from another shower, this time without company, though I certainly had it before the shower. I can't help wonder if she knows. I remind myself that she has a boyfriend and likely wouldn't give a shit how I spend my free time, but having spent every night at her place, watching shows and listening to music and eating together, for nearly a week now, my extracurricular activities don't sit right.

Then again, neither does the fact that she has a boyfriend.

She leans back, smiling as she tells me about the progress they're making on the new sector of the shell. "We have most of the bracing up, so they're bringing someone in from engineering to run the backup oxygen system," she says. "It'll be nice to ditch the respirators after that. I can't wait to get rid of that thing."

"You still wear them?" I ask.

"Yep," she says, drawing her feet up onto the couch.

Her knees come to rest atop my leg, her feet drawn up against her butt. I debate whether to put an arm around her or let my hand rest on her knee, but she's wearing shorts again, and bare skin feels too… intimate. More so than Sheldon would likely appreciate at any rate, though no where near what I'd like. In the end, I settle for leaving my arm exactly where it is on my lap.

"They had a power surge in a new sector a year ago," Kira says. "The primary life support went offline for a while. A few of the mechs were unconscious when medical got to them with respirators, but one was too far into the new sector."

Her voice grows quiet as she says, "She didn't make it. So, we wear them just in case."

A chill settles over me as I realize how dangerous her job here is. I'm planting seeds and digging in the dirt, harvesting crops.

Sure, farming accidents happen sometimes, but so do industrial accidents. At least I don't have the added danger of being in an outer space construction area.

Kira leans forward, peering into my face. "You okay?"

I search her gaze, let my eyes trace her long lashes, her full lips. "I just hadn't realized how much danger your job meant you were in," I say, voice hushed. "I just… I lost my mom, my dad, the farm… I don't want to lose you too."

The words feel like too much, too much to admit and too much to put on her, but they're already out in the air. I can't call them back.

Her features soften, and her molasses eyes flit between mine. She looks at my lips for half a beat, just long enough to stop my heart in its tracks.

Then, she leans into me, pulling my arm around her shoulder and putting her hand on my chest. She moves her thumb in slow strokes, and my other arm goes around her, too.

"Why don't they have you wear space suits in there?" I whisper.

"Because there's oxygen and gravity and atmosphere," she says with a soft laugh. "There are a lot of layers to the shell. They do apparently have people wear full space suits if they have to go into the outer layers of it though. I won't be allowed to even tour those layers until after I've been here about a month, and even then, I'll only be getting a tour. Unless there's an emergency, only senior mechs do repairs up there."

I let out a breath, grateful for that at least.

"I've always been a stickler for safety," she says. "I start each day fully intending to walk out of my shift of my own volition and with all my pieces fully intact. Okay?"

I nod, but I can't shake the fear of losing her to a power surge or an equipment malfunction or a falling beam. Only the solid warmth of her in my arms starts my heart beating again.

"Want to talk about your dad?" she asks. "Or watch one of his messages?"

My chest collapses, and I bow my head forward, resting it atop hers. And though I'm not sure I can stomach the sight of him breathing his last breaths or saying his last words... I don't know that I can stand to put it off much longer.

So, I nod, head moving against hers. "Is that okay?"

"Of course," she says, sitting up straight and reversing our roles, pulling me against her so that my head rests on her shoulder.

I issue the commands in my mind, and my Link does the work, painting his image across her wall. I expect him to be lying in a hospital bed, hooked up to all the machines from when I was there, but he's sitting in a chair by the window in his room. Dust clouds the air beyond and clings to the glass in streaks from a recent rain, sharply contrasting the sterile white room and the crisp, grey chair.

He looks even more frail than I remember. His skin sags as if it's barely hanging onto his bones, and his eyes are gaunt. My heart twists at the sight.

He looks to someone off camera, asking, "Is it ready?"

When he looks to the camera again, a smile brightens his face, and in his eyes, I see the ghost of the man who raised me. The fervor for life, the stubbornness, the willpower that meant he never gave up on anything.

My chest bucks.

"Hey, Jordie," he says. "I know we said our goodbyes already, but I didn't want you to think I forgot about you. I've been awfully busy, but I couldn't forget you."

A laugh from off camera tells me who stands in the room with him. Deanna, an orderly on the evening shift, spent a lot of time with him, playing card games when I was working on the farm.

"Busy keeping us all on our toes," she says.

My dad shushes her. "Don't tell everything you know," he says, laughing.

But the laugh turns quickly to a coughing fit, and my chest tightens.

Deanna bustles forward, bringing over the oxygen mask he *should* have on, but he shakes his head.

"Not while I'm talking to my boy."

She puts her hands on her hips, staring him down, and if anyone could out-stubborn him, it'd be her. But he shakes his head, still coughing.

"Won't be long," he says between coughs. "I need to do this."

A chill settles over me. Kira tightens her arms around me, and her breath hitches.

Slowly, the fit abates, and my father sits up straight once more. When he speaks again, his voice is raspy, and Deanna tries to hand him a glass of water. On this, he relents, sipping carefully with shaky hands, spilling a few drops over his stubbled chin. She takes the glass, moving out of view again, and Dad looks straight into the camera, peering into the depths of my soul.

"There are some things I need to tell you, Jordie. I know you felt bad leaving, but I want you to know I'm proud of you for going," he says, and my throat grows thick. Tears prick at the corners of my eyes. "I'm real proud of you. Your mama would be too. Not many people get to go, but you, my little

Jordie boy, you're good enough to be there. You *deserve* to be there, and I don't ever want you to forget that."

I suck in a deep breath, but it catches, nearly turning to a sob.

"You wouldn't hear that kind of talk when you were here, stubborn as you are," he says.

"I wonder where he got that from," Deanna says, voice thick with tears even as she jokes.

Dad smiles. "One of life's great mysteries." Then, he grows serious again, and the grey pallor of his skin becomes more evident by the second. "It's time for me to go be with your mama though, and you needed to hear it from me before I go. I'm having them give me the shot tomorrow morning."

My lungs heave, and tears spill over.

He turns, gazing out the window at the dust-filled sky that never quite brightens even at noon. "This isn't a world I want to be in," he whispers, then turns back to the camera. "I just had to hang on long enough to get you out of it and onto better things. But your mama and me will always be with you. I'm proud of you, Jordie boy. Love you."

A sob breaks me, and Kira wraps her arms tighter, pulling me against her as the message ends.

***

My thoughts scatter as Annetya moves against me. I bury myself deeper, coming apart, and she collapses onto the table. She gasps for breath, back heaving beneath me, and I grip her hips tight, holding her backside against me.

And still, my mind is blank.

Empty.

Peaceful.

The graceful line of her spine, the curve of her backside, her smooth skin, the grip she has on my body as she pulses around me… It chases away the agony that digs talons into my heart nearly every waking second.

I breathe hard, coming down from our tryst, and she lets her weight rest on the table, the sides of her breasts barely visible on either side of her ribs. Leaning forward, I rest my head on her shoulder, bracing my arm on the table, covering her with my body for a moment as we catch our breath.

Then, I slip free of her, fastening my jeans. Panting, she takes a moment longer to push herself up to standing.

"Goddamn," she whispers, pulling her jeans up.

I chuckle, body loose and mind awash with ecstasy.

She turns to face me, leaning back against the table, and my eyes roam her bare breasts for a moment. Stepping forward, I nip at her neck as I reach past her for my shirt. She arches, nipples pressing against my chest, and a shiver rolls through me.

But I pull back, chuckling again.

"Tease," she says.

"I'm not sure *that* was a tease," I say, gesturing to the table.

She tosses her head back with a laugh, then grabs her bra. "Fair enough."

We dress quietly after that. She moves through her apartment, washing her hands in the bathroom, and I do the same when she's done.

But before I leave, she asks, "Any word on whether Kira's boyfriend is coming up here or not?"

I go still, halfway to the door, and turn to face her. "How'd you know her boyfriend might be coming here?"

"Word travels fast," she says with a look that says I should've known. "If she were single, she'd be fighting guys off with a stick. I guarantee she'd have just as many propositions as you do."

A flicker of jealousy moves through me, and I school my features quickly. But not quickly enough.

"And that's why I'm asking. I've seen how you look at her," Annetya says with a smirk.

I stammer, trying to figure out how to tell the woman I've just slept with that I might be falling in love with someone else.

Annetya laughs though. "It's fine, relax. This isn't a relationship. You're not my type."

Deadpan, I stare at her.

"Not my *relationship* type," she amends with a laugh. "We don't have much in common that I'm aware of, certainly not a sense of humor." Then, crossing her arms, she goes on. "Do you watch true crime?"

I shake my head. "No. Sci-fi or fantasy stuff, cooking shows, sitcoms. Never true crime."

"I hate all things sci-fi and fantasy. Same with cooking shows. Sitcoms are okay, but dramas are better," she says.

"Agree to disagree."

"Do you read thrillers?"

Again, my answer is a no. "Sci-fi and fantasy."

"Gross," she says, and my jaw drops.

"Music? I like hip hop, specifically the early stuff from the 1990s and early 2000s," she says. "You?"

"I hate hip hop. Rock, metal, that sort of stuff. Jazz metal is amazing. It really got good in the early 2300s. Karenin Vestiny really reinvented–" I cut off at the pure, unadulterated horror shining in her eyes. "What?"

"I hate jazz and metal, and the thought of combining the two makes me irrationally angry," she says.

I laugh, head falling back. "Seriously?"

"Seriously," she says. "And none of that matters for what we're doing here. You and I are just two single adults having fun. I just want to know if that's going to change any time soon so I know if I should start looking for someone else. Which brings me back to my first question. Do you know if he's coming up here?"

I blink a few times, staring at her. Finally, shaking my head, I say, "I don't know. I haven't asked her. It feels… weird to ask."

***

Two of Kira's work friends, a man named Akimitsu and a woman named Anaiah, sit with us in a restaurant close to the new sector. They talk about a job they're working on as Kira rises to her feet to go get our food.

"Want some help?" I ask, getting up before she even answers.

"I guess I could use some extra hands," she says.

"Well, I can't do surgery to give you extra hands, but I can carry things."

She rolls her eyes, and the laugh that crosses her lips makes my stomach flutter. We retrieve our food from the counter, and the man behind it eyes Kira's glowing, pulsing Link, then her. His eyes glide over her curves, finally landing on her face, and he smiles appreciatively.

My stomach turns, and my hands ball into fists at my sides as jealousy rocks through me.

But there's nothing I can do.

And no real reason for me to feel this way.

After all, she has a boyfriend. It's not like she's going to sleep with this guy, or me, and I know damn well how I've been spending my time away from her.

Guilt sours in my gut, and I drop my gaze to the trays of food on the counter. Forcing my hands to unfurl, I reach for them, taking mine and Kira's. She takes the other two for her friends.

Finally, the man notices me, giving me a quick nod and a raised eyebrow. He tips his head toward her while she's not looking, and I mouth, "Has a boyfriend."

68

He gives me a sympathetic smile, and I wonder if maybe he noticed me before, noticed the way my hands balled up at the sight of him checking her out.

I shrug, pretending a nonchalance I don't feel, and turn away.

Back at the table, we place the trays in front of the right seats and sit down. She begins eating quickly, but I'm not sure I feel up to food now, even though I was starving before.

I glance out the front windows at the wall I hadn't seen until now. Or hadn't noticed. The illusion of being outside diminished the moment I saw the pale grey metal.

"I told you that weld wouldn't hold," the other woman says.

"How long did it last?" Kira asks.

"Under load? About two seconds," Anaiah says.

Kira rests her head in her hands.

"We lost thirty plant species," Anaiah says.

My head jerks up, and I stare at them. "What species?"

We haven't planted the new crops yet. We were supposed to start planting the new strains of beans that came in on the ship with us soon since we had to clear out the wheat fields first.

"Some trees," Akimitsu says. "It's fine. There's time before the next ship of settlers comes. They already sent a message asking for new seeds on the next ship."

Kira stares at him, just as dumbfounded as I am.

"Guess why he rushed? Just take a guess what he was doing instead of taking the time to do his job correctly," Anaiah says.

I wait, not knowing the man well enough to guess. Though Kira knows him better than I do, she waits as well, still staring at him.

The other woman goes on. "He was hooking up with one of the women on the cleaning crew."

"Wait," Kira says. "You botched your job because you were sleeping around?"

I shrink from her tone, but I'm not sure she even knows about my… activities.

"What? Are you really mad at me over that?" he stammers. "It's not like I'm the only idiot here sleeping around."

He gives me a pointed look, and Kira turns to me, face falling as she takes in my guilty expression. I offer the only defense I can.

"Don't compare yourself to me," I say to him, voice defensive. "I do my job."

"Oh, really?" Akimitsu says, eyebrow raised skeptically.

"You're eating fresh vegetables right now, aren't you?" I ask.

He relents, and we eat, though the conversation is stilted. I contribute almost nothing, sitting silently for most of the meal and eating my food without noticing it.

When we rise to leave, Anaiah elbows Akimitsu, casting significant glances at me and Kira. He pales, but I don't spare him a look, just gesture for them to walk out first. I hang back to walk with Kira, taking her arm in mine to slow her down. The other two move faster, largely thanks to Anaiah.

But Kira stays silent.

She watches her feet, expression thoughtful. As they move ahead and we walk arm in arm, I try to figure out what to say, how to explain, or if I even *should* explain.

Incapable of coming up with anything better, I ask, "What's wrong?"

"It's nothing."

My stomach drops. "It's obviously not nothing. What's going on?"

Still, she says nothing.

"Do you agree with Akimitsu?"

Finally, she looks at me, but confusion draws her brows together. "About what?"

"Me being an idiot…" I begin. Then, more quietly, I add, "Sleeping around."

"I don't get to have an opinion on that," she says, looking forward once again.

She picks up her pace, but I stop, tugging on her arm to turn her toward me. My hand rests gently on her bicep, and she meets my gaze reluctantly.

"You do, actually, get a say on that. You're pretty important to me," I say, before fully realizing the truth I've just given her. Clearing my throat, I go on. "Unlike when he says it, if you say I'm being an idiot, I actually give a shit."

She opens her mouth, then closes it. Looking down, she says, "You're an adult. You can do what you want, sleep with who you want." Her voice cracks on the words. "I don't get any say in that."

She takes a few steps backward, arm slipping through my hand as she moves away.

Chapter Eight

Kira

Kristoff hands me a rag to wipe grease from my arm, and though it leaves a black smudge in its wake, most of it comes off. I offer it back, and he shakes his head.

"Hang on to it. We'll be back on this shit after lunch. You'll need it again," he says.

I tuck it into the back pocket of my jeans, letting it hang partly out. "Fair enough."

I survey the disassembled crank system, eyeing the bearing that prompted this whole job. Or at least, I eye what's left of it. The little, metal balls within it have all gone missing, scattered and rolled away when the housing came apart.

"I guess we'll hunt those bearings down after lunch too?" I ask. Most of the shops I worked at back on Earth would've let them disappear, left them to gather dust under shelves or in cracks in the floor, or just swept them into the trash since they're likely scratched or cracked. But I assume here, they'll be repurposed or melted down or used for… something.

Kristoff nods, patting me on the back with a hand turned black with this morning's work, his tattooed wedding ring nearly obscured. "You learn quick. Let's go eat for now. Want to join Mina and me? I'm meeting her at the cafe around the corner."

"Maybe. I'm meeting my friend, Jordan, there," I say. "I'll see if he minds some extra company."

We wash our hands, then meander out of the large freight elevator shaft. Kristoff closes the doors, fixing his lock onto them. A tag stating the area can't be opened by anyone but him hangs from it, a safety precaution we followed at a factory I was contracted to once. Everyone had their own locks for any job they worked on.

"Will I get my own locks?" I ask.

"Once you're out of your adjustment period, yeah. While you're working with a senior mech for every job, it's up to them to lock out whatever you're on," he answers.

I nod, and then, we're off, moving through the halls of the maintenance area outside the elevator shaft. We pass the motorized carts used to haul large crates from the airlock above to the elevator, then to the roads outside. I trail a hand over the steering wheel of one that looks like it's seen better days.

"Ole Kirsha's been here since the first ship," Kristoff says, patting the back of the cart's seat. "She's a little rough around the edges, but she's tough. You just have to know how to work with her."

I eye the dings and dents in the cart's sheet metal panels, the scrapes and scuffs in her safety yellow paint, the worn finish on the buttons and levers. Dipping my head in a silent salute to this machine that came to space before me, I follow Kristoff outside.

He keeps up a steady stream of conversation, telling me about his wife, their three kids, and the fourth baby on the way. My spirits lift at the normalcy of it, the parallels with life back home.

When we approach the cafe, he points out a petite woman with thick black hair pulled back and a hand on a little baby bump. "Alright, kiddo," he says, putting an arm around my shoulder. "Prepare yourself. She's going to ask a lot of questions."

I laugh, stomach flipping at the nickname.

Kiddo.

Was Akimitsu right? Is he going to… What did Akimitsu say… Papa Bear me?

I look up at him, at the hints of grey sneaking in at his temples, at the crow's feet edging his eyes when he beams at his wife. And though he isn't much more than fifteen years older than me, I don't think I'd mind a place under his wing.

Mina turns to us, eyes sparkling when they land on me. For a moment, I fear she may think his arm around my shoulder means something else, but she only laughs.

"Another for the brood?" she asks him when we're close enough, and though she speaks Common, a light Chinese accent hangs on her words, just like a faint Russian accent hangs on Kristoff's.

I guess my Common probably has an American accent.

"You always wanted a big family," he says, releasing me to kiss her.

Her smile widens, and she leans into him for an instant. Standing straight, she hugs me, introducing herself. "In case he forgot to mention, I'm Mina."

"He did mention that. He told me a lot about you," I say, gazing into warm brown eyes. "I'm Kira."

Pulling back, I hold myself apart once more, suddenly feeling like I always did when families came to the orphanage to pick out a new kid. I squirm inside, hating that I still don't feel like I'll ever measure up.

But Mina smiles and opens the door to the cafe for me, and Kristoff tucks me under his arm again, pulling me along.

Jordan waits inside, already seated at a small table since the couch is occupied. He sees me, face falling when he takes in Kristoff's arm around my shoulder, but then, his eyes color with some other emotion, something that looks like guilt. My heart flies through a maelstrom of emotions, too quick and jumbled for me to parse them out. It settles on warmth at the sight of him, and I smile as we approach.

"Mina, Kristoff, this is Jordan. Jordan, this is Kristoff, one of the senior mechs, and his wife, Mina. Mind if they join us?" I ask. Then, with a chuckle that

I hope hides how much I actually want it, I add, "Apparently, I'm part of their brood now."

Jordan furrows his brows, lips curving upward as he stands. "Part of their what?"

Mina eschews his outstretched hand, moving around the table to hug Jordan instead. "Our brood," she says. "Kristoff has a habit of collecting kids."

Jordan laughs, finally hugging her back. He tries to shake Kristoff's hand, but receives a hug from him as well.

"And don't argue about being too old to be our kids," he says. "You're practically babies here. Newborns, birthed from the ship."

I throw my head back with a laugh, and though Jordan shakes his head, his eyes dance with mirth.

***

As we eat our food, Mina does indeed ask a lot of questions. She splits her time, interrogating me for a while, then Jordan, allowing one of us to eat while she questions the other. Jordan explains about his parents' deaths, about the farm going to their neighbor, and about the girls he never had time to date.

And then, she turns to me again.

"So, how about you? Let's get it all out there and done with," she says. "Was your family glad you were selected?"

I open my mouth, then close it. Glancing down at my soup, I shake my head. "I never met my family. Grew up in an orphanage."

At least it was easy to leave them behind, I guess.

I don't look up because I don't want to see the awkward uncertainty on their faces as they try to figure out what to say. I don't want their pity or their platitudes.

"Fuck 'em then," Kristoff says, and my head jerks up. I stare at him, open mouthed. But he goes on. "We're officially your family now. We do dinners on Saturday nights. Everyone brings something, so we have lots of food."

My heart stutters in my chest.

Mina looks to Jordan and says, "That goes for you too."

And then, both our Links flash the bright, vivid blue of a new message before returning to the subdued blue pulses of old messages.

"That's our address," Mina says. "We eat at seven, but if you're off and want to come over early, you're more than welcome."

I almost argue, almost tell them they don't have to bother, don't have to include me, but I stop myself just shy of speaking the words. Because I want this. I want to belong, want someone to want me around.

And though I pushed people away on Earth all the time, the chill that hasn't quite left my bones from cryosleep only goes away in moments like this.

Moments with people.

Some small part of me wonders if maybe it isn't a physical chill, but a mental or emotional chill, some sort of psychological aftermath of leaving everything and everyone behind, however few my attachments may have been.

So, even with butterflies in my stomach and the gut-wrenching fear that they'll find me lacking once they get to know me, I say, "I'm in."

A glance at Jordan finds him nodding. "Me too."

But when I lean against him, where he was quick to do so yesterday, he hesitates before putting his arm around me.

***

Jordan disappears into his apartment to shower, and that same cold feeling falls over me. I swallow hard as I open my door, pushing myself through the motions of getting cleaned up and pretending that I don't hope he'll come over to sit with

77

me again tonight, pretending I don't want him to stay over again.

The door closes behind me, and I move to the bathroom, stripping my clothes off quickly. I toss them into the hamper and step into the shower, begging the hot water to chase away the chill. But my suspicion earlier might've been correct, because even when the steam fills the room, nearly choking me, even when my skin burns beneath the scalding water, I'm still cold.

I wash and step out. Pulling out an oversized t-shirt and some shorts, I dress and settle in on the couch.

I can't pretend I don't want Jordan here, but I have to be fair to Shel, even if he's already seeing someone else.

After a moment of wondering how it works and a quick search of the net, I prompt my Link to record me.

"Hey, Shel," I begin. "I… I don't know if you'll be selected. You probably will, but when you get here… I don't think we should see each other anymore. I haven't watched all of your messages yet. I know I should've…"

I trail off, casting my gaze around the room.

"But it's weird here. Not the place itself, or the people, but being here, not being on Earth. It's… a lot. I'm going to watch the rest of your messages regardless, I owe you that, but I think I need to move on. I think you should too."

Then, I cast about my mind for an appropriate way to end this message. Finding none, I simply say, "Bye, Shel," and end the recording.

A weight lifts from my chest, and my eyes fall closed. I don't miss Shel the way I should, the way I would if I actually wanted to be with him. I haven't missed him since getting here and don't regret ending it the way I thought I might.

But it's another tie severed, another bond with the old world broken.

And a chill sweeps through me.

I send the message, then start figuring up how long it'll take for it to get there, but I stop myself short.

It doesn't matter how long it takes. It's done.

Rising to my feet, I comb my fingers through my hair, shaking it out. Before I even realize what I'm doing, I slip on some flats at the door and open it, intending to go to Jordan. My door opens to voices.

Jordan's voice and a woman's.

"Annetya said you might be able to help me out," the woman says, voice low and sultry.

"She did, did she?" he asks with a low chuckle.

"Mmhmm… She said you were very, *very* helpful," this strange woman says.

Heat blooms over my cheeks, and humiliation and anger war within my gut.

"Can I come in?" she asks him, voice barely audible, muffled as if said with lips pressed to something, some part of Jordan.

"I thought that was my job," he answers, voice deep and husky.

My stomach drops.

The woman laughs, a throaty sound, and his door closes with a soft click down the hall, cutting her off.

My eyes prick. Retreating back into my apartment, I curl up in my bed. My stomach turns, and I tug the blanket up over my head, covering my ears.

But I won't hear them, won't hear him with her. The soundproofing here is state of the art, just like everything else.

Tears well up, and trickle free. They cascade onto the pillow as my mind spirals.

Is that all he wanted from me when he tried to kiss me?

But I thought…

He wouldn't *have curled up with me if that was all he wanted, right?*

But it doesn't matter.

He's with her, and I'm as alone as I've always been.

It doesn't matter.

He's my friend.

The soft blue of my Link pulses, reminding me that I have messages from Sheldon, and while I don't relish the thought of what they might contain, I could use the distraction. Moving my arm just a bit further away from my face, I prompt my Link to play the next message.

Shel appears, apartment a mess. The woman from the previous message sits on the couch with him, legs over his lap as she naps, or pretends to. I don't miss the artful arrangement of her limbs, the tilt of her head that's obviously meant to show off the graceful curve of her neck. Posturing, marking her territory.

Again, she wears his shirt and nothing else, and the bottom buttons were just too much to bother with. It hangs open from her waist, showing me the side of her hip.

I roll my eyes, even though his behavior still stings. Maybe we weren't great together, but I did everything for him, and he couldn't respect me enough to keep it in his pants for even a week after I was gone.

But it doesn't matter now. I've already ended it. My spirits lift, just a little.

Haven't I always been better off alone?

But I can't believe that lie anymore.

Shel puts one hand on the woman's knee, letting the other rest atop her shin. She shifts, arching her back, and I know she isn't actually asleep.

"My tests are taking longer than yours did," Sheldon says, voice laced with bitterness. "They're being more thorough now. There's no other explanation, no other reason they wouldn't want to send a perfectly healthy doctor."

He shakes his head, as if scoffing at the very idea of them testing him to begin with rather than simply sending him along.

I check the time stamp on the message and see that it was sent a month after I left. The air leaves me.

A month.

He went weeks without sending anything.

My eyes drift out of focus, and I stare at the bed sheet beneath me for a moment. The video pauses automatically when it senses I no longer pay attention, but that doesn't prompt me to go back to it.

Another realization dawns.

A month.

He'd already been in testing for a month and a half when I left. He should've only had a week before they called him to a Coalition Facility for flight preparation and cryo-fitness testing.

But he's still at home after a month.

Are they being that thorough?

Or are they not sending him?

***

A knock at my door pulls me up from the couch. I dismiss the book I was reading on my Link and cast a glance at the wall I share with Jordan's apartment. The woman's voice from earlier comes back to me, and I dismiss the thought of it being him at the door.

Maybe the counselor from the building is introducing themself?

I pad across the floor on bare feet, t-shirt brushing my thighs past the edges of my shorts. Briefly, I consider putting on something more appropriate, in case it is the counselor, but if they're making house calls, surely they expect to find people dressed comfortably.

At the door, I signal my Link to open it, but it isn't the counselor. Jordan stands in the hall, beard still damp from a shower.

Another shower.

"Hey," I say. "I didn't know you were... I mean, I thought you had..." I stammer, unsure of my next words. Finally, I just finish with, "...Company."

His cheeks color unexpectedly, and he looks down at the floor. "I did," he says. Then, meeting my gaze again, he adds, "But it wasn't anyone I wanted to actually spend time with, just..."

His words settle over me, and though warmth fills my veins for a moment, it's chased away quickly by the thought of that woman. Stepping back, I let him in, closing the door behind him.

"Sorry," Jordan says. "I didn't mean to... I mean, I meant what I said, but I don't want you to feel awkward. I know you have a boyfriend–" he turns, leaning back against the counter and smirking, "–even if he's not the best."

"It's not awkward. And... I don't actually have a boyfriend anymore. I just sent him a message a little bit ago," I say. Then, because it feels awkward not telling him how I knew he had company, because I don't want him thinking I was listening through the wall or something, I add, "I was going to tell you earlier, but you were talking to someone else in the hall, so I just read for a while instead."

I don't look up to see Jordan's face, just walk past him to settle on the couch. He stands in the kitchen, leaning against the counter, for a few more heartbeats. The silence stretches out, and before I begin fidgeting, I signal my Link to resume our–

The baking show.

Not *our* show.

It begins to play, and though he hasn't joined me on the couch, I don't pause it. The bakers and the hosts fill the silence that stretches out between Jordan and me.

After nearly a minute, he crosses the small space, settling in next to me. The tiny couch keeps him close, but he doesn't put his arm around me automatically, not like he did earlier.

But then, he hesitated earlier.

And the woman in the hall said someone else told her to go to him.

The room blurs as my eyes drift out of focus once more. I nod slowly, realizing that he must've been with this Annetya woman earlier today, that she's likely the reason he hesitated at lunch, the reason he looked guilty when he saw me.

But we weren't together, *aren't* together.

I had a boyfriend.

Guilt twists within me, even as my heart aches. I remind myself that Jordan and I barely know each other, that we aren't together and he doesn't owe me anything.

As the show progresses, moving through the various stages of the competition, he doesn't move closer or put his arm around me. But as the day wears on us both, we slump into the cushions.

When my head falls to his shoulder and my eyes drift closed, I barely feel it as he shifts, leaning sideways and pulling me with him. His hand slips beneath my knees, lifting my legs onto the couch, and then, we're laying together again.

His warmth seeps into my body as his arms come around me, and I breathe deeply of the fresh scent of his soap.

He smooths my hair back behind my ear and whispers, "I'm sorry."

Sleep rises to claim me, turning the words I try to say into an incomprehensible mumble.

Chapter Nine

Jordan

I keep my head down at work, thankful not to work with Annetya for the day. Not that there'd be much room for talking, let alone… other things. I swing my scythe, taking down the wheat crop I glimpsed on my first day. A man named Yeshua works on one side of me, with his wife following behind to bundle the wheat he cuts. Aarya follows me, doing the same.

Beyond Yeshua, a few more teams work steadily.

On my other side, a woman named Elise swings another scythe. She casts coquettish glances my way, leaning into her French accent whenever she has cause to speak. Her tan skin shines in the light, and the way she tries to stay ahead of me, to stay in sight, makes me wonder if Annetya talked to her too.

Sighing, I bend to my work, swinging the scythe yet again, stepping forward, wishing all the while I hadn't given myself over to this again yesterday. Apparently, with no news from the world back home, people have nothing to talk about but this, and it's gotten away from me.

Guilt and regret spread through me, and Kira's face last night fills my mind. She tried to hide it, but hurt tightened her eyes as she mentioned me having company.

And I'd only just missed her.

She broke up with Sheldon. She was coming to my apartment.

But Greta got there first.

My stomach sours, and I slash through another patch of wheat, letting the golden stalks fall sideways for Aarya to bundle.

✳✳✳

By lunch, we have half the field done. The stalks stand in the field, bundled and drying out. Though it would've been done differently on Earth, with tractors and specialized equipment, the sight of the field half taken in with bundled stalks standing tall the way our ancestors would've left them before tractors were common, is beautiful.

My eyes rake over our work, and I swipe a hand over my face, wiping sweat away before it can fall into my eyes. Again, I adjust the respirator straps that aren't there, and Aarya chuckles.

Elise touches my arm, laughing warmly. Long, blonde locks fall in graceful curls from her ponytail, draping over her shoulder. "You'll get used to being here," she says, leaning into the touch.

I step away, saying, "I know. I'm going to go meet Kira for lunch now."

Elise tips her head to the side, considering me, but I don't try to parse out the expression on her face. Turning, I move through the field, heading toward the nearest pickup station.

But she follows.

"Are you sure you don't want to spend some time together first?"

"I'm sure," I say.

"Sorry, it's just that, well, Annetya said…"

I don't even look at her. "I know. But I'm good now."

She puts her hands up in my periphery, and I force myself to stop. Turning, I say, "Look. There's someone I want to actually have a relationship with, and that won't work if I'm doing… this. It wasn't an option before, so I've been *doing* this, but now it might be. Okay? It's not you."

The hurt in her hazel eyes falls away, replaced by understanding, and she nods.

86

"Well, if it doesn't work out, come find me. You've got most of your year left," she says with a wink.

Shaking my head, I chuff out a laugh and walk away.

***

At the cafe near our apartment building, Kira already has my food waiting, having sent a message asking what I wanted. She sits at a table, sipping at her tea and staring at her Link. As I walk up behind her, I notice a man on the screen, sitting in an apartment with dust-streaked windows.

It must be Sheldon, one of his messages.

My stomach twists, then drops completely at the sight of a woman on the couch with him, both barely dressed. Dropping my gaze, I move around her to the opposite side of the table. She looks up quickly, dismissing the message, and meets my gaze.

"Hey," she says with a smile, but the word is tentative somehow.

"Hey," I say, sitting down with my salad and soup.

"You got here quick," she says. "I wouldn't have been watching one of Shel's messages, but I wasn't expecting you yet."

Guilt churns within me at the thought of what delayed my arrival to our lunches in the past, but I merely take up my fork and poke at my salad. "I didn't get caught up at work this time," I say.

And though I didn't say it, she seems to know what held me back before. Emotions flit across her face, too quick to discern, and I slide my free hand closer to hers on the table. Lightning crackle in the space between us, and my heart races.

She tips her hand toward mine, brushing her finger over mine. Bolts of electricity surge through me, and my breath catches. Swallowing hard, I hold her gaze as I take her hand.

87

Her smile widens, and color builds on her cheeks.

Looking down at her food, she eats quietly, and so do I.

Chapter Ten

Kira

As we walk to the transport station, Jordan puts his arm around me, tucking me against him. I slide an arm around his waist, and heat flows through me, so much fiercer than the warmth his presence usually affords me.

"Have you, I mean, do you know if Sheldon's coming up here yet?" he asks, voice hesitant.

I take a deep breath, lungs filling with the scent of him, all earth and woodsy somehow, and I wonder what cologne he wears. But I have to answer his question.

"Well, even if they select him, I won't be with him," I begin, getting what feels like the important part out first. "But after that message… I don't think they're going to. They're doing a lot of extra stuff that they didn't do for me, extra tests I mean, and he still wasn't in a Coalition Facility. He was in testing for a little over two months, as of that message anyway. How long were you in testing?"

The transport station comes into view as he thinks through his answer, and I glimpse a woman he works with, whose name I'm not sure I know, sitting on one of the benches. She eyes us through the glass with a curious expression.

"Not including the time they spent going over my background and medical history before calling me in for tests, I think a month before they moved me into the Coalition Facility. Maybe a month and a half, tops," he says.

I nod. "I think it was the same for me. I don't think they're going to send him here, not if they still haven't called him in."

Jordan pulls me closer, bending to press a kiss to the top of my head, and heat pools in my stomach. When we reach the transport station, he takes in the woman on the bench, body going just slightly rigid against my side. I glance at him, but already, he's schooling his features.

"Jordan," she says, dipping her head in greeting. "This must be Kira."

He nods, swallowing so hard I hear it. He sits on a bench across from her, beneath the glass overhang of the transport station, and lays his arm across the back of it. I nestle in beneath his arm, sitting close.

"Yes," he finally says. "Kira, this is Annetya."

My stomach drops as I take her in, from the slim waist emphasized by her tight t-shirt to the dark hair falling over her shoulders to the jeans that hug shapely legs. The woman from the other night said Annetya sent her. So, this woman clearly knew he was willing to sleep around, even orchestrated liaisons with other women.

And from his rigid posture, I'm sure she was with him.

The color drains from my face, and I drop my gaze. Jordan tightens his arm around me, and though I lean into him, my stomach turns.

When my transport back to the shop arrives, my heart tears in two. Relief at escaping the awkwardness wars with reluctance to leave him with her.

Jordan gets to his feet, walking me to the door of the transport that's only a step above the motorized carts from the shops. In place of the flatbed that sits behind the two seats of our carts, it has eight more seats, and rather than a steering wheel, it has a computer terminal programmed with travel routes.

Jordan's arm moves to my waist, hand on the small of my back, and he opens the door for me. "See you at dinner?" he asks, voice tinged with hope and anxiety.

My eyes flick to Annetya, but he doesn't flinch. So, I nod. Meeting his steel grey eyes, I find relief and the same hope that filled his words.

I climb aboard the transport, surreptitiously watching out the window as he sits back down to wait for his. Annetya moves to sit next to him, and my insides twist. But when she puts her hand on his knee, he lifts it, setting her hand in her own lap, and scooting a friendly distance away from her.

And despite myself, I breathe a sigh of relief.

Chapter Eleven

Jordan

Annetya looks at me, eyes pensive. "Her boyfriend isn't coming here then?"

Settling back into my seat, I shrug. "Don't know for sure, but she doesn't think so. She still hasn't watched all of his messages." My shoulders feel lighter as I speak my next words. "Whether he does or not doesn't matter though. She sent him a message breaking it off."

Annetya nods, turning to watch the road instead of me. "Make a move yet?"

"Not yet. Not really," I say, though holding her hand earlier and agreeing on dinner felt... significant. "I figure I should put a few days between sleeping with someone else and asking her out."

Annetya laughs under her breath and says, "The honorable thing to do."

I laugh with her. "Of course."

"Alright. I'll start looking for someone new. There were fewer single people on your ship than on the last one, but I'll find someone," she says, crossing her legs at the ankles.

"Are you going to tell the others, or am I spending the next few days letting them know?"

"I already sent them a message. I'll send another letting them know you were going to talk to them so they don't think you're an ass or anything," she says.

Again, I laugh. "Thanks."

The transport heading to the fields rolls up, coming to a stop, and we climb aboard. I take a seat, and she moves a few rows back, sitting with a man that came here on the Cutlass with us. His Link still

pulses a soft blue, and I shake my head, laughing quietly.

94

Chapter Twelve

Kira

At dinner, we sit at a large table in the cafe, surrounded by a few people from work, and Jordan scoots his chair close enough to mine that our thighs brush when either of us shifts. A trickle of heat builds within me, pooling low in my belly as we eat and laugh with friends neither of us knew just weeks ago.

Kristoff opens his mouth to speak, but Termana shakes beneath us. A chill runs through me as everyone goes still. Even the people cooking in the kitchen stop, and an eerie silence falls over us all. Fear chills my heart.

"What was that?" Jordan asks, hand sliding over mine.

He laces our fingers together, and I squeeze his hand. Shifting closer to him in the chair, my thigh presses to his.

And then, my Link, as well as those of everyone I work with, light up. The urgent red color fills my veins with ice. I stare down at the thing, lit up like some sort of curse object from a fantasy movie.

Across from me, Kristoff stands, saying, "Take your food with you. Eat on the transports."

He gathers his utensils, setting them on his plate as my Link reads the message to me, parroting it through my cochlear implant.

"An S-type asteroid struck the Shell, causing moderate damage in sectors three and four. All Mechs are to report for emergency duty as soon as possible. This is a level three alert. Collapse is not imminent. I repeat, collapse is not imminent. However, immediate repairs are necessary. Report to your sector workshop. Your supervisor will inform you of your duties."

"Shit…" I whisper, pushing myself up to my feet.

"Why didn't the MagShield stop it?" I ask Kristoff.

"It's an S-type," he says. "Stone. Mostly silica and rock. It doesn't have much metal, if any, so the MagShield can't calibrate to repel it."

"Wait, that was an asteroid hit?" Jordan asks, color draining from his face. He stands beside me, helping me gather my utensils.

A woman from the kitchen rushes out, helping pack up our food and drinks. My heart races. Her hands shake as she tries to put a lid on my drink, and I take it from her, hands steady as ever. Kristoff notices, nodding his approval.

Beside him, Akimitsu spills his drink, clearly rattled, and Mina casts nervous glances at Kristoff. He touches her cheek, kissing her gently on the forehead, then, with a deep breath, he grabs his food.

"Come on then," he says to Akimitsu and me.

I turn to Jordan, about to say goodbye for the night, but he puts a hand to my lower back.

"I'll walk you out," he says.

Nodding, I turn and follow Kristoff to the nearest transport station. Jordan sticks close to my side. His hand never leaves me, and warmth emanates from that point of contact, chasing away the trill of fear slipping through me.

As we walk, Akimitsu glances up at the Shell, over and again. His eyes spend nearly as much time ticked upward as they do watching where he's going, and his hands still shake.

"You're not going into the Shell, are you?" Jordan whispers.

Up ahead, Kristoff answers for me. "No. She's not. She and Akimitsu are going to take over for Ikemba. He's helping engineering install the oxygen recyclers in Sector Nine. He's going up into the Shell with me and the senior mechs from other Sectors. Anaiah's going to be in the shop, near the elevator, in case we need anything."

Jordan and Akimitsu breathe out twin sighs of relief.

"You're good though, Kira," Kristoff says. "You'll be doing what Anaiah does soon enough."

Akimitsu drops his head, rubbing a hand over his face. His cheeks color, and he blows out a shaky breath.

The transport station comes into view, and two small carts I've never seen before turn the corner up ahead, coming our way. The two-seated things approach quickly, far more so than the larger ones.

"Emergency transports," Kristoff explains when I ask. "Faster, smaller, programmed for specific routes when they're needed and dispatched *only* when needed."

I nod, then stare up at Kristoff. His ruddy cheeks are flushed, but not with nerves. Maybe exhilaration.

"Be careful," I say, heart twisting at the thought of losing the closest thing I've ever had to a father figure. Even if it's only been jokes about him taking me in. Even if I haven't been to one of the family dinners yet.

"I will," he says. "You too. Respirators the whole time."

I answer in the affirmative, having never considered going without my mask in that sector, not after Anaiah's story about her sister.

He squeezes my shoulder, then Akimitsu's, then climbs into his transport. Before closing the door, he tells me, "Ikemba is already on his way to the elevator. Engineering is waiting for you in Sector Nine."

And then, he's off.

I set my food and drink on a seat in the transport station and turn to Jordan, taking a deep breath. Akimitsu climbs aboard our transport, but I slip my arms around Jordan, pulling him close.

"Be careful," he whispers, arms tight around me and hands balled up around my shirt. His voice breaks under the strain of his concern, and I hold him tighter, insides warming and flipping.

"My part of this is no different than any other work day," I say. "I've been in Sector Nine a lot. I don't take my respirator off until I'm back in the airlock. I promise."

He pulls back, searching my gaze, hands coming up to cup my cheeks. His eyes drop to my lips for the barest instant, and my heart stutters.

"I'll be okay," I assure him. "Just a normal day at the office for me. Kristoff and Ikemba are doing the dangerous stuff."

"People get hurt doing what you're doing all the time," he says. "Industrial accidents have always been a thing."

I nod, unable to argue with that. "I always do my best to walk out of work with all my parts intact, remember?"

He swallows hard, then nods slowly. "Okay. Come to my place when you're done. I don't care what time it is."

I smile as my heart does somersaults in my chest. "See you soon."

He takes a deep breath, then releases me, stepping away reluctantly. I take my drink and food in hand and climb aboard the transport.

Settling my food on my lap, I lift my hand in a wave as we pull away. He smiles, though it's tinged with worry, as he waves back.

Then, since there's nothing else to do on the ride to Sector Nine, I finish my food. But as I eat, a message from Kristoff comes through to my Link.

"Keep an eye on Akimitsu. He gets nervous under pressure. Never had a problem back on Earth, but the stakes are higher here."

I take a deep breath, finally nervous, but not about my job. I don't look at Akimitsu, don't want to make it obvious that the message was about him.

But I pay more attention to him in my periphery.

And he doesn't look like he's handling this well.

***

Akimitsu watches the Shell as I work with the people from Engineering, two men named Haruto and Abdul. They fiddle with little wires and thick cables, hoses and vents, and I bolt the machines down, fixing braces and extra supports into place where necessary.

I climb aboard the platform the oxygen recyclers rest upon, arms streaked with the oil that coats the brand new parts. Reaching between the recyclers, I strain to tighten a bolt, but my ratchet smacks the side of an I-beam on one side, and the tank of the recycler on the other side. Moving in eighth turns, I let out a sigh of frustration.

This one bolt is going to take all fucking night.

Snaking my arm out and sitting back on my haunches, I call down, "Hey, A."

He doesn't answer, merely stares up at the Shell in abject terror.

"Akimitsu," I call, a little more insistent.

This time, he turns to look at me.

"Mind passing me the extension?" I hold up my ratchet, then say, "3/4 inch drive. I need the long one."

He doesn't crack a joke at my wording, as I'd expected. Hell, as I'd hoped. He merely nods, moving in slow, halting steps to the tool box. The extension shakes in his grip as he comes back and hands it up to me.

My brows come together as I pop the socket off and fit the extension into place. Reattaching the socket, I look Akimitsu over. His pale skin looks sallow, and his breathing is shallow.

"Do you need medical?" I ask him.

He shakes his head. "I'm fine."

When I ask again, he gets defensive. "It's perfectly normal to be afraid right now. The fucking ceiling might collapse on us and jettison us all into outer space. I'm not the crazy one for being afraid. You all are just... fucking robots."

I arch a brow, and he kicks the tool box, sending its contents jangling and scattering across the floor.

"I called medical," Abdul says. "I sent a message to your supervisors, too."

"What the fuck is wrong with you?" Akimitsu demands. "I'm fine. Don't get them involved. In case you forgot, they're busy making sure we don't all die!"

Haruto looks at me over the oxygen recyclers, then offers, "I'll go down and sit with him."

But as he tries to find a way to hand over all the wires and cables he'd been attaching, he finds no way to lay them down without them getting hopelessly tangled.

"Attach those first," Abdul says. "Akimitsu says he's fine. Get those attached before you go down there."

He sends a private message to Haruto and me though. "He's okay for now. The first time he got this nervous at an asteroid hit, he started throwing things. He was better the last two times, but stay up here until medical comes for him."

"That's right! I'm fucking fine!" Akimitsu yells, and the words echo through the empty Sector.

Okay, then.

Getting back to work, thankful the extension is long enough to reach over the shallow tank of the recycler, I make quick work of the bolt, then the next five as well. And as I work, I ask, "How often do asteroids hit the shell?"

Haruto speaks, voice quiet and deliberate as he attaches the wiring harness. "Not very often now. In the early days, while they were still mining the ones closest to Termana, it was more common. Mostly small bumps and scrapes though. Only one came close to puncturing the outer Shell."

"Almost everything nearby has been mined out of existence now," Abdul says. "There are only a few asteroids close, and most are M-type, so the MagShield keeps them at a safe distance."

I nod, and they keep talking in quiet tones, soothing tones, telling me about how much safer things are now, though I suspect most of that is for Akimitsu's benefit. When the sound of an approaching transport grows clearer, I lay down my tools and look over the edge of the platform.

Akimitsu stands with his hands twined and placed atop his head. He breathes deeply, chest rising and falling deliberately.

He glances up at me and says, "Sorry," before walking away to meet the medical transport.

I send him a quick message. "It's no problem. This place is a lot. Just get to feeling better."

∗∗∗

A few hours later, after washing the oil and grease from my hands and arms, I climb the stairs of our apartment building. I consider getting a full shower before going to Jordan's, but I stop at his door rather than going to my own. My hand rises to knock, and in seconds he opens the door. His arms wrap around me instantly, and I chuckle softly as I hug him back.

"I'm okay, I promise," I say. "Just a normal day at work. Except for Akimitsu."

I pull back a little. "You're going to get covered in oil," I say. "All the new parts are coated in it. I only washed my arms and hands so far."

101

I gesture to my coveralls, turned down to my waist. My shirt escaped the grease thanks to them, but the coveralls themselves have a fair amount on them.

But Jordan shakes his head and pulls me against him again. He whispers, "I don't care about grease."

A small laugh escapes me again, but I sink into his embrace, arms sliding around his waist. I rest my head against his chest with my forehead pressed against his neck. Heat builds within me, and my heart races.

His hands splay over my back, one on my shoulder blade, the other on the small of my back, and I relish the contact. My body buzzes. His Adam's apple bobs as he swallows, and I slide one hand to the side of his neck.

My Link flashes bright blue as a message comes in, and we pull back just a bit. Blushing, I glance at the screen to find that it's from Kristoff.

"We got the Shell repaired. Good work in Sector Nine. I didn't want to send Akimitsu with you, but standard protocol is to send two mechs to take over for a Senior, and the night shifters were asleep. You did good though."

My shoulders fall, and I breathe out a sigh of relief. "They got the Shell fixed."

Jordan sags, head coming to rest atop mine. "Thank the stars," he whispers, breath moving my hair.

I touch his neck again and say, "I'm going to get a shower. Come over after?"

He nods, searching my gaze again. "Okay. You can tell me what happened with Akimitsu."

I start to pull away, then think better of it. "Do you… I mean, you could hang out at my place while I clean up."

Fire burns my veins as I imagine asking him into the shower with me. But I don't want to be like the other women he's been seeing.

Annetya's hand on his thigh flashes through my mind before I remind myself that he moved her hand.

Maybe…
Maybe that's done?

He closes his door, hand sliding into mine, and we walk the few steps to my apartment. And though I know what I feel for him is more than just friendship, I can't bring myself to start something if he's still with them.

***

As I towel off, I let my Link play Sheldon's last message, letting the audio play only through my cochlear implant. Water droplets roll down back, dripping from my hair, as he takes shape on the screen.

Pacing back and forth, he fumes, and I fill my lungs with steamy air.

They aren't sending him.

He shakes his head, still pacing, and his anger makes me certain. No sense of dismay or loss overcomes me though.

Finally, he stops, staring me down through the camera. "You're just a fucking welder! You play puzzles with scraps. That's it!"

He shakes his head again.

"They deny me, a goddamn doctor! And yet, they took *you*. You've gotta be fucking kidding me." He spits the last words, pacing once again. "When was the last time you saved a fucking life?"

And though he'll never know it, I know the answer to that question.

Today.

In a way, I saved lives today.

I did my part, did my job, installing oxygen recyclers. I took over so Ikemba could repair the Shell, and in that way, I helped keep us all alive.

Sheldon turns to the camera once more, jabbing his finger in its direction. "Fuck you!" he shouts. Then, he calls out across the apartment. The woman from the prior messages comes in, looking concerned. But he walks up to her, taking her in his arms, and says, "Let's show that bitch what she left behind."

He rips his shirt off her, exposing her bare breasts, lacy underwear, and slim legs. Their mouths meet, and she arches against him.

I shut the message off.

Chapter Thirteen

Jordan

I lie on Kira's couch with her curled up in my arms, one leg thrown over me. She wakes slowly when her alarm goes off, rubbing her eyes as she yawns. My eyes roam over her face, and I smooth her hair back.

"How long have you been awake?" she asks.

"Not long," I say, though I've been up nearly half an hour.

"You should've woken me up."

I laugh softly. "No way. You had a long day yesterday, and you said you didn't have to work until nine today."

She glances at her Link, then groans. "I have to get up," she murmurs, though she puts her arm around me again.

Chuckling, I say, "You seem thrilled about that."

She shakes her head, burrowing against my chest, and a trill of fire moves through me. Breathing deeply, I try to keep myself under control.

Her chest puffs out against mine as she takes a big breath, then she presses a gentle kiss to my chest. My heart stutters.

Pushing herself up, she says, "I really do have to get up. You're off today, right?"

She sits on the edge of the couch, fingers combing through her long, dark hair, and I barely stop myself from staring.

Clearing my throat, I answer. "Yeah, I'm off work today. It's going to be weird." My first day off here, we were off together and hung out most of the day. "I'm not sure what I'm going to do all by my lonesome."

She casts a wry look my way, but I see the question in her eyes as she asks, "All by your lonesome, huh?" Her teasing tone almost disguises the genuine curiosity.

With all the sincerity I can muster, I say, "All by my lonesome. At least until you're off work. I might just go back to bed for a few hours, see what it's like to sleep in for once."

She laughs. "I wish I could. You're more than welcome to hang out here if you don't want to walk the incredibly long distance back to your place."

Chuckling, I shake my head. "I need to brush my teeth. Even if I go back to sleep, that has to happen."

I sit up, fully aware of how close she is now, backside pressed to the side of my hip. She waves a hand in front of her face.

"I see why you want to brush your teeth," she says with a laugh.

Rolling my eyes, I nudge her shoulder. "Ha ha, very funny."

She rises to her feet, hips swaying as she walks away. "I know. It's a shame they don't have a comedy club or something. I could do stand up."

"Slow down there," I say. "One joke does not a comedian make."

She casts a look over her shoulder, eyes twinkling, and my heart skips. "Are you sure about that?"

Her tank top hugs her waist and shows off her strong arms and shoulders. Shorts show off muscled legs, and her gaze makes my blood run hot.

Drawing a deep breath, I say, "I'm very sure. See you at dinner?"

She nods, then turns back to the cabinets in the kitchen. "Family dinner at Kristoff and Mina's tonight, right?"

"I forgot," I say. "That is today, isn't it? I guess I'll figure out what food we can bring while you're working."

She doesn't correct my use of the word 'we,' doesn't insist that we're separate. "You sure?" she asks. "I'm off at 6:30. I can help."

"If you're off at 6:30, that's enough time to shower. That's about it. I'll have food ready to go," I say.

She eyes me, hand going still on the sink handle. A little smile tugs at the corners of her lips. "Thank you," she says before filling a glass with water.

I move through the kitchen and put a hand to the small of her back as I pass. "No problem," I whisper by her ear, then step past her. "Be careful at work today. I'm going to go sleep for a while."

She laughs. "Lucky."

When I look back from the doorway, she's watching me, smiling. I return the expression and duck out into the hall, forcing myself to leave before I go back in and press her to that counter, before I make her late for work.

Before I screw this up and make her think sex is all I want with her.

***

Attempts to sleep in prove fruitless. Years of rising before the sun pierced the dust clouds mean that even here, even far away from Earth and the dust, I only manage another hour of sleep after leaving Kira's apartment. I settle in with a snack and a book, passing the morning with more leisure than I've managed in most of my adult life.

But I grow restless by lunch time.

My eyes drift up from the screen of my Link, leaving the book behind, and I stare out the window at the world humanity built to replace the one we destroyed. A strange mix of hope and despair flows through me, and a chill creeps into my soul.

But this time, instead of finding someone to sleep with, I get up to start working on the food we'll take with tonight. After all, homemade bread takes a long time, and the thought of making one of Mom's recipes, the memories of working in the kitchen with her before she died, chases that chill away.

***

Warmth spills from the oven as I take the bread out, and my head fills with memories of home. I smile at the thought of my mother baking bread for my father and me, at the memory of sitting down to eat a slice of it slathered with the butter our neighbors made, at the thought of my parents gazing lovingly at each other as they held hands and ate their portions.

My heart warms, and I settle the baking pans on the cooling racks, all of which came to space with me. Passed down through my family for a few generations, they're pieces of my great grandparents and grandparents, pieces of my parents, that haven't been forgotten or left behind on Earth. They're pieces of the best times in our home.

I lean on the counter, gazing out the window. A knock at the door draws me upright though. Checking the time, I trail a hand over the cooling racks as I pass.

I open the door to find Kira and barely suppress a laugh. Grease coats her arms and stains her shirt. Smudges of it streak her face.

She arches a brow at me, and I lose the battle. A laugh bursts from me.

She shakes her head. "Ha ha," she intones, voice dripping with sarcasm, but her lips turn up at the corners. "I just wanted to let you know I had to clean up before dinner."

Struggling to contain my mirth, I say, "I can see that."

She rolls her eyes.

"Let me know when you're ready. The bread should be cool by then."

She considers me, growing slightly more seri-ous. "I didn't know if you'd want to wait or go on ahead," she says.

"I'll wait. Especially since I'm only being pulled into the brood by association," I tell her.

Shaking her head, she says, "Kristoff and Mina liked you. And apparently, they adopt everyone they like." Backing toward her apartment, she smiles. "You're stuck, with or without me."

And though I like the idea of having a warm group of people to fall in with, I like it a lot better with her.

Chapter Fourteen

Kira

Laughter spills through every room of the house except the room occupied by the children. They play a game that seems to consist only of roaring and fake explosion noises. The cacophony grows quieter, muffled, and a moment later, Anaiah reappears, coming to sit with her wife, Jess.

"Sorry," Anaiah says. "They're a little excited. Apparently, they learned about explosions in science class this week." She rolls her eyes, slipping am arm around Jess' shoulders. "The door's shut now, so we might hear ourselves think for a little while."

"Where's the fun in that?" Akimitsu asks, getting up from the table. His Link flashes, and music plays from around the room.

"Aki," Mina says, chiding, though he only increases the volume.

"Don't make us put the child locks on the net again," Kristoff says. He adjusts the volume to a more reasonable level, and for a moment, we just sit, talking and listening.

"Wait. Isn't this Vietnamese?" Jess asks, suddenly.

Akimitsu nods. "My grandmother on my Mom's side was Vietnamese. This was some of her favorite music."

"Isn't it from forever ago?" Jess asks. "Your grandma can't have been that old."

"Maybe she was immortal," he says, arching a brow.

I stare at Akimitsu, barely suppressing my laughter. I can't help appreciate the music though. When it shifts to a slower song, I glance at my Link, but since I don't know the language, I don't expect the title to make sense. "em bỏ hút thuốc chưa by Bich Phuong" shows on the screen, and the words make no more sense than I expected them to. My Link offers to translate them, but Jordan takes my hand, rising to his feet beside me, pulling my attention away.

"Want to dance?"

I stare up at him, heart skipping at the thought, but also slightly embarrassed. No one else is dancing. My eyes dart around to the others, all absorbed in conversation except for Anaiah. Her gaze moves between Jordan and me, then searches my face before getting to her feet.

She pulls Jess up, saying, "Jordan has a good idea. Come on."

Laughing, Jess gets to her feet. "What are we doing?"

"Dancing."

I don't hear the rest of what they say. Turning back to Jordan, I swallow. He stands, patient, still holding my hand.

"Do you even know what they're saying? I don't know this language," I hedge.

"I don't need to know the words to feel the music," he says.

Blushing furiously, I take a deep breath and rise to my feet. I don't look at Akimitsu or Kristoff, can't bring myself to meet Mina's gaze.

Jordan pulls me to the open part of the room, though it isn't very big. His arms slide around my waist, and though we've been this close while sleeping, this feels more intimate somehow. My hands move up his chest to his shoulders, then around to the back of his neck. Our eyes meet as our feet move, and for half a breath, everything else falls away. I search his grey gaze, swallowing hard.

Akimitsu whoops, and my blush deepens. I bury my face in Jordan's chest, and his arms tighten around me. But as I peek over his shoulder, I see that the whooping wasn't for us.

Anaiah and Jess spin, and Jess dips Anaiah. They come back together, and Jess pulls Anaiah's leg up, hand on her thigh. Their smiles loosen my shoulders, and I relax into Jordan's embrace. We sway gently as the song swells, and heat moves between us. Tension crackles through me.

The song draws to a close, and applause rings out. I step away from Jordan, standing beside him with my eyes downcast. But we weren't the ones putting on a show, so thankfully, the ovation isn't for us.

Anaiah and Jess take a bow, and when Anaiah meets my gaze, I mouth, "Thank you." Because I'm certain that show was for me, to take the attention away from us. She smiles, confirming my suspicion.

Jordan leans to whisper in my ear. "Want to step outside for a second?"

Nodding, I follow him into the kitchen, pretending I don't notice the significant glance between Mina and Anaiah as they watch us slip away. We move through the little kitchen, and my eyes trace the drawings from Mina and Kristoff's children, hung on the fridge. A few from Anaiah and Jess' kids hang there too, as well as drawings from the child of a couple that couldn't be here tonight.

Mina's artwork brightens the room with cozy landscapes from a version of Earth none of us knew, hung on the wall opposite the counters, and little knick knacks sit atop the counter between appliances. The kids' shoes lie deserted by the back door. The last slice of Jordan's bread lies on the counter next to the dishes the others brought, some empty, some with a portion or two left in them.

And the whole room feels warm.

Jordan opens the door for me, and we step out into the night air that isn't real night air. But it feels like the way it was in old movies.

A little crisp.

Dark except for the streetlights and the glow from windows.

Far above us, only the operating lights of various support systems still shine, and if I don't look closely, don't try to figure out which system they're part of, they almost look like stars sprinkled through the heavens.

I lean against the banister that borders the small porch, gazing out at the golden silhouettes the neighbor's lights make of the kids' toys in the backyard. Jordan stands close, hand resting on the small of my back, and heat flows from his touch, joining with the soothing warmth of this evening.

"I'm sorry," he whispers.

I turn to look at him, brows coming together. With a shake of my head, I ask, "For what?"

"For… Annetya. For Greta. For…" He trails off, drawing a deep breath.

"You don't owe me an explanation," I say. "Like I said before, that's not something I have a say in."

Even if it stings.

Even if my heart wrenches in my chest at the thought.

"I haven't… I haven't been with them," he says. "Not since you broke up with Sheldon."

I freeze, staring at him. Suddenly, the beautiful night lighting irks me because I can't see the look on his face, only the barest hints of it as the light from the street reaches for us.

But he turns to face me, and the light from the kitchen window shows me earnest grey eyes and a hopeful smile. My breath catches.

"They aren't what I want," he says, stepping closer. "They never were."

I swallow hard, searching his gaze, and the answer I want plays in the depths. Still, I ask, "What do you want?"

He smiles, warm and tender, and his hand rises to the side of my neck. My heart thuds, pulse roaring beneath his fingertips, and his thumb traces my jaw.

In a husky whisper, he says, "You."

He leans forward, and I meet him, lips brushing over his, arms wrapping around his neck. Fire burns through me, and he tangles his hand in my hair. Our mouths move, and he presses himself against me, free hand clasping my waist.

Sliding one hand to his neck, I pull back, breaths coming fast. My lips spread in a smile.

Mouth moving against mine, he asks, "I assume that means you"re okay with going on a date?"

Chuckling, I rest my forehead against his. "Yeah," I say. "I'd like that."

His lips find mine once more, sweet and gentle this time, and he steps backward, pulling me with him. "Let's get back in there before Akimitsu comes out looking for us."

My smile widens, and though I'd like to stay out here with him, he's right. Akimitsu would look for us before anyone else.

We step inside, and the cozy kitchen wraps around us again. The voices of people who want to be my family spill from the next room. The tension of never knowing if I belonged slowly melts away, and though I may doubt it later, I can't right now.

We settle into our chairs in the dining room, and Jess begins filling us in on a story we missed the beginning of, but all our Links flash an alarming red. My blood runs cold, and I glance at my Link.

An emergency transmission from the Survival Coalition waits.

"I'll play it on the wall," Kristoff says, voice hushed.

The main wall of the living room, left bare despite the artwork everywhere else, glows to life. A woman in a dark, button-down shirt appears, face streaked with tears. Her make-up runs, and it takes me a moment to realize it's Minister Pria Khatri. Her normally composed features now sit in a mask of sorrow and horror, and more tears fall.

Drawing a deep breath, she wipes at her face and sits up straighter. The woman who sent countless messages across the world, the Minister of Human Affairs, reappears, pulling her composure out of thin air.

"This will be the last message sent from Earth," she begins. "At 6:37a.m., the core of the London Nuclear Reactor, the fourth largest in the world, reached critical failure."

My stomach drops as gasps sound throughout the room. A chill descends over me.

"As we all know, the atmosphere has been severely… disrupted… ever since the formation and eruption of the Mount Seleni volcano and the eruption of Mount Vesuvius years ago. This latest catastrophe has pushed the atmosphere beyond anything we can likely recover from. The ash already present in the air, as well as the nuclear fallout, will send the planet into a winter that few will survive." Her voice grows quiet as she adds, "If any."

Her eyes drop to her hands, and she takes another fortifying breath. My eyes dart to the wall behind her, wondering why it's painted such a dark shade.

But it isn't.

It's a window, and the world beyond it has gone dark.

She coughs, and suddenly I see the sickly pallor to her skin, not just the draw of emotion and stress.

How close was she to the meltdown?

Close enough to survive, at least initially.

"Carry us with you," she whispers. "You're humanity's last hope. I'm going to sit with my family now."

The screen goes dark, reverting to a wall once more, and I swallow hard. A stunned silence falls over us all, and I take Jordan's hand in mine. He squeezes hard, but I don't flinch, merely squeeze back.

I glance around at the family I've found here, glad I've finally found a place for myself, glad I made it here.

Because it looks like we're the last settlers on Termana.

Other Books by this Author

The Regonia Chronicles

Awakening
Faltering
Ascending
Reckoning

Literary Fantasy Novels

Soul Bearer
The Gem of Meruna
A Heart of Salt & Silver
A Blessed Darkness
Allmother Rising
The Sword and The Savage

Literary Thriller Novellas

Annabelle
Things Left Unsaid

Literary Post-Apocalyptic Novel

World for the Broken

About the Author

Elexis Bell is a quiet nerd with too many hobbies, including everything from gaming to shower-singing and even archery, weather permitting. She specializes in sarcasm and writing stories that make people feel. She's made a home for herself with her husband and a small army of cats.

She writes dark, gritty stories, sprinkling gut-wrenching emotions over high fantasy romance, thrillers, post-apocalyptic romance, and science fiction.

For further information, follow her on Instagram, Twitter, or Facebook, or check out her blog on her website. There, you can sign up for her newsletter to stay up to date on all future book releases, giveaways, and ongoing projects.

www.elexisbell.com